THE ROYAL
PREGNANCY TEST

THE ROYAL PREGNANCY TEST

HEIDI RICE

MILLS & BOON

First published in Great Britain 2020
by Mills & Boon, an imprint of HarperCollins*Publishers*
1 London Bridge Street, London, SE1 9GF

www.harpercollins.co.uk

HarperCollins*Publishers*
1st Floor, Watermarque Building, Ringsend Road
Dublin 4, Ireland

Large Print edition 2021

© 2020 Heidi Rice

ISBN: 978-0-263-28835-3

To Natalie Anderson,
who is an absolute sweetheart
to work with and a brilliant author too.

PROLOGUE

PRINCESS JUNO ALICE MONROYALE braked the hired snowmobile and wrenched up her goggles to take in the stunning view. Snow fluttered down, coating the Alpine landscape in pristine white, framing the ornate turrets and gables of a sixteenth-century castle perched on the clifftop across the gorge. The defiant structure looked magnificent against the gathering dusk of a December night. Like a cartoon fantasy made real.

Home.

Juno's heart butted her tonsils and the cold air clogged her lungs.

Had it really been eight and a half years since she had visited her homeland and seen her twin sister, Jade—the Queen of Monrova—in the flesh?

Why hadn't she come back sooner, much sooner?

But even as the question echoed in her consciousness, the disastrous events of the summer she had turned sixteen came hurtling back.

'Kiss me, Leo, you know you want to.'

'Why on earth would I want to kiss you? You're just a spoilt brat. Now leave me alone, or I shall suggest to your father he give you the spanking you clearly deserve.'

Heat rose up Juno's neck, warming her chilled skin.

She could still hear the amused contempt in King Leonardo DeLessi Severo's voice, still see the bored superiority in his blue eyes, still feel the inappropriate goosebumps as he'd grasped her wrists in firm hands and dragged her arms off his shoulders.

Good to know the memory of that summer night—when she'd thrown herself at the King of Severene at the Monrova Summer Ball and been brutally rejected—still had the power to make her cringe, big time.

Quite impressive really when she considered all the other cringeworthy moments she'd accumulated over the last eight and a half years—the most recent being the social-media snafu in her new job, which this last-minute trip into her past had been a handy way to avoid.

Some things never change.

She tugged her goggles down, and revved the snowmobile's engine.

Forget about it.

She wasn't going to think about that last disastrous summer in Monrova or the mistake she'd made a couple of days ago in New York in her new job at Byrne IT. Luckily it wasn't *that* big a screw-up and the big boss, Alvaro Byrne, knew nothing about it. It would all have blown over long before she got back to New York.

Juno headed across the gorge towards the unused entrance to the palace she and Jade had discovered during the summers they had spent together in Monrova after their parents' divorce.

But as she located the path etched into the cliff face—*result*—she couldn't seem to stop her mind from drifting to the past again.

Those summers had been so precious after she and Jade had been separated as eight-year-olds. They'd been so happy, so excited, at the chance to reconnect for two months each year, once Juno had been forced to live the rest of the year in exile in New York with their mother, Alice, and Jade—two minutes older and therefore the heir to the throne—had stayed with their father, King Andreas, to be instructed in her role as the future Queen. But as the years had passed, and Juno's life in New York had become increasingly chaotic, she'd found it harder and harder to live under her father's strict rules, and not drag Jade into mischief with her.

That cringeworthy moment with Leo had been the last straw—once her father had found out about it. Juno shivered as she manoeuvred the snowmobile along the narrow path, every single word he'd said to her that day—and the cold, flat disapproval in his eyes—still fresh…

'If you can't behave yourself in a manner befitting your status, I will have you returned to your mother in New York immediately. Do you understand me? Each summer your behaviour gets worse. You're insolent and disobedient, a bad influence on your sister, and now you've disgraced the Crown by behaving like a hoyden and throwing yourself at King Leonardo. You're becoming as much of a liability as your mother.'

Of course, she'd told her father where he could shove his ultimatum, because she'd been hurt and humiliated and struggling desperately not to show it. But the chilling way he'd nodded and then had her removed from the palace—without even giving her a chance to say goodbye to her sister—still haunted her.

No wonder she hadn't returned to Monrova while her father was still alive. Had he ever even loved her?

Shuddering, she brushed away the tear that had seeped out from under her goggles.

Jeez, Juno, dial down on the drama, before you end up freezing your eyeballs.

It didn't matter now. King Andreas had been dead for over a year. And today she was returning on her own terms—to surprise her sister.

Jade was the ruler of Monrova now. Jade with her serene sweetness and her full open heart. Jade who loved her enough not to see Juno's many faults.

Juno huffed out a laugh as she took the final bend in the path and spotted the wrought-iron gate she had been looking for.

Bingo.

She was coming home for Christmas and nothing—not memories of Leo's brutal rejection or her father's final punishment or even her own impressive ability to screw up on a regular basis—could stop her.

All she had to do now was get to her sister's suite of rooms in the palace's West Wing—where she knew Jade would be chillaxing before tonight's Winter Ball—without being spotted by the royal staff.

And for that, she had a cunning plan.

Twenty minutes later Juno approached her sister's suite, astonished her plan—to pretend to be the Queen—had actually worked.

Decorated in garlands of fir and holly and red and gold satin ribbons and sprinkled with fairy lights, the ornate salons and sitting rooms she passed looked magical and mysterious dressed in their Christmas finery, the way she remembered them as a child.

The scents familiar from her last Christmas at the palace as an eight-year-old—fresh pine sap, wax polish and cinnamon—seared her lungs, but she refused to let the wave of nostalgia derail her.

Reaching the suite she had once shared with her sister, she opened the door.

Every one of her fondest memories slammed

into her as she spied her sister, sitting on an antique Chesterfield sofa in front of a roaring fire reading a novel. Jade's vibrant hair, so like Juno's own, haloed around her head, the cascade of chestnut curls lit by the lights from the expertly decorated tree in the corner of the room.

'Jade,' she said, her voice a rasp of emotion.

Her sister's head lifted. 'Juno?' she whispered. 'You're… You're here?'

The hope and longing in Jade's tone wrapped around Juno's heart. And joy blindsided her.

'Yes, but keep your voice down, I'm here incognito.'

A bright smile ripped across Jade's face as Juno's demure sister dumped the book on the floor and leapt out of her chair.

Juno's heart pounded so hard and fast it hurt, as her sister flung her arms around her. She absorbed the comforting scent of vanilla, for the first time in what felt like for ever. Tears stung her eyes and she hugged her twin back, as tight as she could.

Their shared laughter echoed off the luxury furnishings and seemed to make the fire in the hearth and the sprinkle of lights on the tree burn brighter.

I'm really home, at last.

'It's so, so good to have you here. Finally.' Jade laughed and tucked her feet under her butt as they settled together on the sofa.

Her sister seemed ridiculously pleased to see her, but Juno noticed Jade was thinner than she remembered her, and even more serene. Perhaps too serene, her calm reserve more ingrained—almost like a shield.

'It's good to be here,' Juno said, and meant it.

'How long can you stay? Please say you can attend the Winter Ball tonight? I'm sure we can find you a gown. It'll be so much more fun with you there. Do you need food? Tea? Wine? Champagne?' Jade asked, her excitement as infectious as her grin as she reached for the smart device used to summon the palace staff.

'No!' Juno lurched forward to stop her sister. 'Let's wait to tell them I'm here. That's why I sneaked in. I wanted to surprise you, but I thought we could spend some alone time before everything goes nuts.'

'Wait a minute… Do you mean *no one* knows

you're here?' Jade put down the keypad. 'How did you manage that? Perhaps I should have a word with my Chief of Security.'

'Simple.' Juno wiggled her eyebrows. 'I snuck in via our secret entrance, then I just pretended to be you.'

'You're joking?' Jade pressed her fingers to her lips.

'Not joking, it worked like a charm too.'

'Juno you are unbelievable,' her sister said, astonishment turning to admiration. 'And you haven't changed a bit.'

'About the Winter Ball,' Juno said. 'I suppose I could come. But why don't I turn up unannounced?' she added, already enjoying the joke. 'Everyone will think they're seeing double.'

See, Father? Still not behaving in a manner befitting my status.

'That's brilliant...' Jade's grin widened. 'Except...' She hesitated, the grin disappearing and her excitement deflating. 'Except King Leonardo is going to be there as the guest of honour. He might not find it amusing.'

What the...? Was this some kind of test? Or a sick joke? Why did *he* have to be here?

'Leo the jerk's here?' Juno said, hoping Jade couldn't see the blush heating her collarbone.

She'd never told her sister about that disastrous attempt at seduction on her last night in Monrova, and she never would. Her mortification did not need company.

'King Leonardo is not a jerk, Juno.' Jade's smile softened. 'He's a brilliant diplomat. A conscientious and extremely intelligent ruler. And a...' Her sister paused and Juno spotted the flicker of doubt cross Jade's face. 'He's a good man even if he has sowed a few wild oats.'

'A *few*?' Juno shot back. 'The guy's a player. He hasn't sowed a few wild oats, he's sowed enough to put an industrial grain conglomerate to shame since he became King...' Two months before Juno had developed that ill-advised crush on him...

'That's not true,' Jade said, protesting a bit too much. What was going on here? 'He's curbed his romantic engagements in the last few months and—'

'Hang on...' Juno interrupted, recalling the avid press speculation recently about a 'fairy-tale marriage' between King Leonardo of

Severene and Queen Jade of Monrova. A rumour Juno had dismissed as hype. Jade had never mentioned Leo in all their email and text conversations over the years, not once. Because Juno would have remembered. 'Why is Leo the guest of honour? You're not…?' Why wasn't Jade meeting her gaze? 'The rumours aren't true, are they? You're not actually dating him?' Juno hissed.

The thought of her sweet, kind, gentle and totally innocent sister hooking up with Leo the man whore was the literal definition of leading a lamb to slaughter.

'No, we're not dating. I don't…' Her sister's blush subsided. 'He's good-looking, I suppose, but we just don't click.'

'Well, thank goodness for that,' Juno said, the twist of horror in her gut releasing a little. Although she had to wonder if her sister was blind.

Leo might be an arrogant jerk but, unfortunately, he'd only become more impossibly attractive in the years since she'd fallen for his dark charms.

At twenty-two, he'd been moody and magnetic and totally gorgeous, at thirty he was even more so. Not that Juno had spent any time perusing the many, many photos of him plastered all over the celebrity press. Much.

'But…' Jade's gaze rose and Juno did not like what she saw, because she knew that expression—stubborn, loyal and scarily pragmatic.

'But…*what*?' Juno said.

Jade sighed. 'But I am considering King Leonardo's offer of a political union between us. Father was in favour of the idea before he died. And the benefits to both our countries are undeniable. A shared heir would…'

'Hold on!' Juno lifted her hand. 'Did you just say shared *heir*? As in a baby? What kind of a political union are you talking about?'

Her sister had the grace to look sheepish. 'A… A marriage.'

Juno's stomach twisted into a pretzel. 'You're not serious?' She took a breath, because she was starting to hyperventilate. 'You just told me you don't even find him attractive. And now you're saying you want to *marry* him and have his *babies*?'

Couldn't her sister see how nuts this sounded?

'*Want* would be too strong a word,' Jade said carefully. 'But I am considering it, yes. Our advisors are strongly in favour of the political union. And we wouldn't have to be intimate to have an heir. There's…' The blush returned. 'Well, there are other ways of conceiving.'

Ways Juno would bet Leo the Player King was not going to be interested in. The guy oozed hotness in every photo and news clip Juno had ever seen of him—even if Jade couldn't see it. No way would a guy like that consider getting his wife pregnant via in vitro fertilisation. Not unless it was absolutely necessary.

'Have you talked to Leo about the other ways?' she asked.

'Well, no,' Jade said, because she really was that innocent. 'We haven't negotiated anything. Yet.'

'Yet?'

'I said I would give him an indication tonight if I was willing to proceed with—'

'Good, so there's still time to stop this madness,' Juno interrupted, her mind working overtime.

She needed to figure out a way to stop Jade from making a decision she could end up regretting for the rest of her life. And fast.

Her sister had been trained for monarchy her

whole life by their father, but there was such a thing as being too dutiful. And considering marriage to a guy you didn't even want to date definitely qualified.

Juno didn't have a lot of experience herself. Contrary to appearances, after Leo's humiliating rejection, too many unwanted advances as a teenager from her mom's handsy boyfriends, and one totally *meh* encounter at high school when she'd lost her virginity, she was not that fussed about sex herself... But surely there had to be more to it than making heirs in a test tube.

And, maybe it was cheesy, but what about love?

'But—' Jade began again.

'But nothing,' Juno cut her off. 'I'm not going to let you do this, Jade. Not for Monrova and certainly not because our father wanted you to. He's dead, you're the monarch now and you're entitled to a life.'

Juno glanced around the room, suddenly seeing the ornate furnishings for what they were, or what they had always been to Jade: a gilded prison. While Juno had lived a chaotic life with their mom on Central Park West, with no boundaries whatsoever, Jade had lived a life of stifling duty with nothing but boundaries.

'A life outside these walls,' she murmured as an idea took shape.

A radical idea that was fraught with possible disaster but also exhilarating and inspired and kind of cool.

Why the heck not?

Jade needed to get away from here—at least for a little while—and get a life. A real life—a normal life. Or as normal as it was possible for either of their lives to be. A life where she got to make her own choices for once—without having to factor in everyone else's priorities. A life where people weren't watching and judging her every second of every day. A life where she could be imperfect, she could make mistakes, and it wouldn't create a diplomatic incident.

A life not unlike the one Juno was busy living in New York.

Suddenly Juno knew, this idea was perfect. A Christmas gift she could give to her sister—as long as she made it crystal-clear Jade didn't have to go into her office.

But how was she going to get Jade to go for it?

'Juno, what are you thinking?' Jade said, a bit too perceptive, as always.

'Nothing,' Juno said, still thinking.

'Really?' her sister asked. 'Because you've got that look on your face you always got before getting us both into trouble.'

Instead of looking concerned at the prospect, though, Jade looked intrigued, curious, maybe even excited—just as she always had when they were children.

And suddenly Juno knew exactly how to sell her bombshell idea to her sister.

Jade had always been one hundred per cent loyal. No matter what, she had always stuck up for Juno when their father went ballistic.

Jade believed Juno would have made a wonderful Queen. Jade was dead wrong about that, of course. Juno would make a disastrous royal.

Perhaps she could be bold and tough when she had to be, but she was more likely to be reckless and impulsive and mouthy—not qualities that made you a shoo-in for the job of monarch or even princess.

But what mattered now wasn't what Juno was *actually* capable of, only what Jade *thought* she was capable of.

'I've had an idea…' Juno said. 'It's kind of nuts, but it'll give you the time and space you need to consider whether you *really* want to marry King Leo the Jerk.'

Or rather the time and space to figure out what a car crash that would be.

'Leonardo is not a jerk,' Jade repeated, but she smiled, the spark of curiosity in her eyes undimmed.

'And it'll give me a chance to see whether or not Father was right to kick me out of the kingdom with Mom,' Juno continued, riding roughshod over the 'Is Leo or Is He Not a Jerk?' debate.

Been there, done that, had my ego torn to shreds to prove it.

'Dad was wrong.' Jade's smile flatlined. 'What's your kind of nuts idea?' she asked, totally taking the bait.

Juno sucked in a breath. *Here goes nothing.*

'I think we should swap places for Christmas.'

Jade's eyebrows shot up her forehead.

'From now until New Year's Eve,' Juno added. 'I'll be the new Queen of Monrova and you can be Princess Pauper of Queens.'

CHAPTER ONE

KING LEONARDO DELESSI SEVERO of the Kingdom of Severene was so bored he was on the verge of lapsing into a coma.

Attending official events such as the Monrova Winter Ball were all part of the job description when you were the ruler of a wealthy European country. That and giving pointless speeches, making dull, dignified small talk, wearing uncomfortable uniforms decorated with too much brocade, and hefting around polished ceremonial swords, which you'd been taught how to wield with rapier-sharp accuracy as a boy but had never had a chance to use.

Queen Jade's financial secretary droned on about the remarkable yield from last year's rapeseed harvest as Leo imagined whipping out the golden sabre banging against his hip and slicing off the feather in the man's tricorn hat.

He stifled an impatient sigh.

Where was the Queen?

The woman was close to an hour late for her own Winter Ball.

He liked and respected Monrova's new monarch. When he'd outlined the benefits of a marriage between them, she had seemed intelligent and engaged, if reserved. She would make him a very suitable wife and joint head of state. Her status and lineage, not to mention her country's abundant mineral reserves, and their similar dedication to civic duty would make theirs the perfect power partnership in the region—plus eventually provide both their countries with an heir. And she was quite beautiful, objectively speaking. There hadn't been much of a spark between them—and he had an unfortunate suspicion she might be a virgin. Her father had often talked proudly of his daughter's 'respectability' before he died, which Leo had assumed was a euphemism for not allowing her to date—and since she had assumed the throne there had been no whiff of any romantic entanglements... Except with him—which he knew to be fiction.

Even if he was hoping to make the rumours a reality.

He would have preferred she not be completely chaste, but he had never had a problem satisfying a beautiful woman, so he didn't see her chronic lack of experience causing too much of a problem once they were wed.

Her tardiness, though, was another matter.

He'd had to exchange more than his fair share of tedious conversation with faceless bureaucrats. And he was starving. His stomach grumbled on cue, the rumble detectable under the tinkle of champagne flutes and the strains of a chamber orchestra in the far corner of the palace antechamber where they were all waiting for the Queen's *late* arrival.

He ignored the flushed reaction of the financial secretary to his increasingly demonstrative hunger pains. What did the man expect? He hadn't had a chance to eat since breakfast due to his full schedule of talks with Monrova's trade ministers.

Talks that the Queen had chosen not to attend because her advisors had said she needed time to 'prepare' for the ball.

If she agreed to become his bride, he would have to make it very clear that delays of this nature would not be tolerated.

A wailing bugle interrupted his internal diatribe, and a royal courtier appeared on the balcony above the antechamber.

About damn time.

A hush descended over the crowd as Queen Jade appeared.

But as she descended the wide sweeping staircase the strangest thing happened. His breathing became a little ragged.

Weird.

He'd considered her beautiful the last time he'd met her a month or so ago. But he had never noticed how lush her figure was before now. The sensual curves filled out the floor-length silver satin ball gown she wore to perfection, drawing his eye to the gown's bodice embroidered in gemstones and her generous cleavage.

He dragged his gaze away as his breathing became laboured. Surprised by his reaction.

Her thick chestnut hair had been arranged in an elaborate up do crowned by a diamond tiara. The headdress's gems glittered in the chandelier light and created a halo that highlighted high cheekbones and the sultry shape of her eyes.

His breath became trapped in his lungs as

the satin shimmered, moving sinuously over her voluptuous figure.

Whatever the hell she'd been doing for the last four hours, it had been worth it.

She looked every inch the Queen, but there was something earthy and elemental and much more approachable about her too, which he hadn't sensed a month ago. Which was even more surprising. He was usually an exceptionally observant man when it came to women. Especially women he intended to marry.

The spark he'd been convinced didn't exist began to sizzle.

The crowd parted and her gaze—bold and direct, and nowhere near as demure as he remembered it—locked on his. Instead of greeting the other, less senior guests first—which was the protocol—she walked past them and headed through the crowd straight towards him.

The sizzle became hot and fluid, sinking deep into his abdomen. The buzz of anticipation in his blood almost as loud as the buzz of conversation building around the room.

Was he actually getting turned on?

Her gaze roamed over him, both daring and amused, and he suddenly had the feeling she was assessing him like one of his own prize stallions. Why had he never noticed that mischievous sparkle before either? It turned the refined jade of her irises to a vibrant emerald.

'Good evening, Leo,' she said, her voice a smoky purr.

The spike of adrenaline was as unsettling as the prickle of surprise.

Every other encounter he'd had with the Queen, she had been exceptionally well versed in etiquette and protocol. She had never even called him by his given name and no one used that nickname…

No one except…

'Kiss me, Leo, you know you want to.'

The shocking memory of bright emerald eyes naked with longing, a voice full of childish demand and adult yearning, and soft fingertips trailing across his nape and detonating in his groin, sent a shaft of déjà vu through his system so uncomfortable he stiffened. The prickle of shame not far behind it.

Not the same girl, damn it.

That had been Jade's twin sister. Princess Juno. King Andreas's younger daughter, the disobedient teenager who had developed a ludicrous crush on him eight summers ago. Ludicrous, that was, until she'd tried to kiss him and—for one split second—he'd been tempted.

He'd been twenty-two and she'd been sixteen. A child and a really annoying one at that. Until that moment in the moonlight, when his libido had played tricks on him—and what he'd seen was the woman, instead of the girl.

He shook off the unsettling memory. The lack of sustenance was obviously messing with his head.

This was the Queen of Monrova. The woman he planned to marry. Not her extremely annoying—and utterly undisciplined—twin. Thank God.

A whisper rolled through the crowd. No doubt the use of the nickname was going to be all over the media tomorrow.

Leo forced a confident smile. 'Good evening, Your Majesty.'

'I hope you haven't been waiting too long,' she added, even though the mocking tone suggested she didn't care in the slightest.

What the hell?

Her breasts rose and fell, the plump flesh

straining against the low-cut gown. But then a flush spread deliciously across her collarbone.

Something hot and volatile stirred, to go with the sizzle that hadn't died. And the forced smile on his lips became genuine. She felt it too, the electric chemistry that had hit him like a lightning bolt.

He gave her a mocking bow and let his gaze rake over her in return.

Whatever game she was playing, he had the urge to play it too.

'Your Majesty, believe me, you were more than worth the exceptionally long wait.' He grasped her fingers and pressed his lips to her knuckles. She shivered—and the sizzle became a spark.

'Shall we?' he said.

'Of course,' she replied, although she sounded less sure.

Touché, Your Majesty.

He folded her arm under his, tugging her against his side to lead her into the banqueting hall.

Even in her heeled slippers, her head barely reached his collarbone, which made her shorter than the women he usually dated. At six foot four, and with a muscular physique, he generally preferred women who didn't make him feel like a giant. But while the size disparity had concerned him before, now he found it a turn-on too.

Perhaps her previously undetected boldness didn't have to be a bad thing?

They entered the large banqueting hall and he tensed.

Fresh holly wreaths elaborately finished with gold ribbons had been hung from the cornicing, while candles burned in the wall sconces to mark the upcoming festive season.

Christmas was his least favourite time of year.

She glanced at him. 'Is something wrong?'

'Not a thing,' he said, surprised she had noticed the slight hesitation. And not sure he liked it.

But when she disengaged her arm as soon as they reached their seats at the top table, he stifled a smile.

Not quite so bold now?

Waving off the waiting footman, he pulled her banqueting throne out.

As she deposited her bottom onto the velvet cushion, an unfamiliar scent teased his nostrils—citrus and musk—which was fresher and more intoxicating than the vanilla perfume he had detected before. His gaze fixed on the spot behind her ear.

Was that where she wore her scent? What would she taste like if he kissed her there? How would she react? Would she writhe? Would she moan?

Before he could think better of it, he whispered in her ear. 'Fair warning, Your Majesty. After my exceptionally long wait, I'm starving.'

She glanced round, her gaze filled with a compelling mix of surprise and awareness. The flush on her cheeks had his mind fogging with lust and his gaze snagged on her mouth. A vision of biting into that plump bottom lip and soothing it with his tongue tortured him.

He drew back, disturbed by the intensity of his reaction.

When was the last time he had wanted a woman so badly he had acted on instinct? His manners were usually impeccable.

Stop staring at her mouth.

'Just to be clear, I'm not on the menu,' she said.

'If you insist, Your Majesty,' he replied. 'Although I consider it my sworn duty to change your mind.'

Her eyes widened—and she frowned. 'Good luck with that, Leo.'

He let out a rough chuckle as the last of his restraint headed straight out of the banqueting hall's large mullioned windows and into the December night.

Game on.

CHAPTER TWO

'I BELIEVE THIS is my dance, Your Majesty. Shall we move through to the ballroom?' Leo bowed, but the formal request was as mocking as the challenge in his crystal blue eyes as they met Juno's.

It was the same challenge that had been tormenting Juno all through several courses of cordon-bleu cuisine.

What the heck had she unleashed? Because whatever this thing was between her and Leo, it was as dangerous as it was unexpected. Unfortunately, it was also exciting.

Leo offered her his arm, the dare in his eyes unmistakeable.

When had she ever been able to resist a dare?

She laid her fingers on his arm and felt the muscles of his forearm tense.

Applause followed them as he led her out of the banqueting hall and into the ballroom beyond—but she could hardly hear it over the pounding of her own pulse.

Leo is a jerk. Leo is a jerk.

Maybe if she kept repeating it, she might remember it.

Because Leo's jerk credentials had become harder and harder to remember through supper, every time he smiled at her with desire darkening his gaze; every time he offered her a taste from his plate like the Pied Piper of seduction; every time he murmured some wry observation and made her laugh; every time he made her heart thunder, or her pulse race or the hot sweet spot between her thighs throb.

Leo might be a jerk, but he was also a superhot and super-charismatic jerk—and now he was giving her the undivided attention she had once craved, he was also super addictive.

They reached the centre of the ballroom at last, the crowd flowing in behind them to wait for their inaugural dance. Leo positioned himself in front of her, resplendent in his dress uniform, an array of medals emblazoned across his chest, his shoulders so broad and strong all she could see was him. Threading his fingers through hers, he lifted her right hand into position as the thirty-piece orchestra played the opening bars of a Viennese waltz, then wrapped his other arm around her waist to draw her into his big body.

Sensation shot up her spine, as his large palm rested on the small of her back, above the low-cut gown. The gown she'd spent an extra hour getting into to make him wait. And to irritate the heck out of him.

While Jade was en route to New York to get a life, Juno had decided her mission tonight was to make Leo reconsider the benefits of a 'political union' with the Queen.

She had thought it would be a cinch. Because eight summers ago irritating Leo had been her super power.

But not tonight.

Tonight every time she opened her smart mouth, made a suggestive comment or attempted some subtle—and some not so subtle—mockery, instead of irritating Leo, she had amused him. And he had only become more attentive.

And attentive was bad, because it only encouraged the impulsiveness that had always been Juno's downfall.

As soon as she'd descended the stairs into the anteroom and seen the ludicrously hot figure Leo cut in his formal clothes, his black hair almost blue, the tempting dimple in his chin making her want to lick it, the shot of adrenaline had become addictive.

And as the night had gone on, it had only got worse.

Because beneath his formal attire and curt mocking manners, Leo had discovered how to neutralise her super power.

No man had ever been aware of her every breath and blush and heartbeat with the same raptor-like focus. No man had ever spoken to her with such respect for her intellect while also relishing, even encouraging, her attempts to outrage and disarm him. No man had ever enjoyed her company the way he appeared to.

And as a result, the only person who had been disarmed was her.

And that had not been the plan at all.

Even as she knew her reaction to Leo was getting out of control, her body swayed in time with his as he swung her round in the steps of the dance. Her breath seized and she got a lungful of his rich exotic scent—starch, salt and subtle, sandalwood cologne.

Her pulse throbbed heavily in her sex—and everywhere his body touched hers—as the lights from the chandelier whirred above their heads.

At last the other guests began to join them on the ballroom floor. The lights dimmed, the dancers glided around in the golden glow of candlelight—their finery as dazzling as the ballroom's ornate rococo design. But all Juno could focus on was the man she clung to.

As the waltz ended, Leo brought them to an abrupt halt in the middle of the room, then leant down.

'Let's get out of here,' he murmured, his breath sending a shiver down her neck. 'So we can discuss our future plans.'

Not a good idea.

'We… We can't,' she managed, disturbed by how much she wanted to say yes. 'I'm the host. I'm supposed to stay till the end of the ball.'

I think!

His lips quirked in the super-sexy smile that had been driving her insane all evening. '*Really?* You're going to play the protocol card after teasing me to death through two solid hours of too-rich food and that never-ending speech from your minister of state?'

'Well… Yes,' she said, stupidly flattered by the thought she'd had the power to tease him at all. 'It will look bad.'

'Jade, honey.' He sighed, cradling her cheek. His calloused palm skimmed over her skin, as his thumb found the pulse hammering in her collarbone. She could feel the eyes of the assembled guests on them, hear the hushed whispers above the music at his forward behaviour. He was making a spectacle of them both, why did that only excite her more?

Was that Leo's superpower—the ability to seduce any woman into compliance at fifty paces?

'We have much to discuss,' he added. 'And everyone will think it's romantic if I drag you away after one dance.'

'But it's not romantic,' she murmured, mesmerised by the challenging light in his eyes as the hot sweet spot between her thighs burned.

'True,' he said, and her chest deflated. 'But that doesn't mean we can't create an impressive show.'

As if to prove his point, he caught her fingers, lifted her hand, opened her closed fist and bit into the swell of flesh under her thumb.

Arrows of sensation darted down, turning the sweet spot into a molten bundle of unrequited yearning. She groaned and he laughed. She tugged her hand free, brutally aware of their audience, but even more brutally aware of the insistent ache between her thighs.

'You wouldn't dare,' she murmured, the challenge issued before she could stop it.

'Watch me,' he said, then clasped her hand and began to lead her through the crowd.

The music had stopped, the eyes of everyone upon them as the guests parted to let them through.

This was madness, but it was an intoxicating madness. The reckless child inside her, who had once sneaked into another ball to kiss him, wanted to see what he would do.

As he headed towards the back of the ballroom, she spotted doors leading onto a balcony that overlooked the gorge, closed now as the snow fell in scatters of white.

It was the same balcony where she had propositioned him all those years ago, at another ball. And been discarded far too easily.

'Wait.' She tugged him to a stop, a laugh trapped in her throat when he shot an impatient look over his shoulder.

'We've waited long enough,' he said. And she had the terrifying thought he knew who she was. That he recognised the rejected girl she'd been. But then he added, 'I thought that waltz would never end.'

'Could we go that way?' she managed, pointing towards the secluded balcony. If he was going to kiss her, she wanted it to be there. Where he'd refused to kiss her all those years ago.

It was nuts, but somehow she felt she owed it to that reckless child. Apparently she still had something to prove to that love-struck girl.

He frowned, his gaze drifting over her ball gown. 'Are you mad?' he said. 'You'll freeze.'

'Perhaps you can find a way to keep me warm,' she said, a little stunned by her own boldness. Her pulse leapt as arousal flared in his eyes.

'Excellent point,' he said, but as his grip tightened and he changed direction towards the balcony doors her sister's chief of staff—Major Something or Other—stepped into their path.

'Your Majesties…' The man introduced himself and bowed low, effectively blocking their escape route.

Juno scrambled to recall his name. Jade had told her who he was in the list of details they'd exchanged that afternoon, about their respective lives, but…

'Garland? What is it?' Leo said, his impatience obvious.

Garland. Hallelujah.

'Perhaps you would both like to repair to King Andreas's former study, so we can discuss…' Garland leaned forward, lowering his voice so their crowd of inquisitive onlookers couldn't overhear '… the latest trade agreement.'

Say, what now? Panic ricocheted through Juno. A trade agreement? Jade hadn't mentioned anything about having to negotiate a trade agreement tonight?

'Queen Jade and I wish to speak alone about our trade agreement,' Leo said.

Relief rushed through Juno as she figured out what trade agreement they were discussing. Otherwise known as the political union with heirs attached. Leo's large hand landed on Juno's hip, his palm skimming over the satin, possessive and provocative. Sensation rioted over her skin.

'But, Your Majesties…' Garland began. 'The advisors are ready to discuss—'

'We can have this discussion without our advisors, Garland,' Leo's commanding voice interrupted.

Dismissed, Garland bowed and turned to leave.

'Wait, Garland, take this with you and give it to my valet,' Leo said.

He let go of Juno's hip, and lifted the ceremonial sword and scabbard he had been wearing all evening over his head. Then handed it to the astonished advisor.

As Garland held the sword, Leo flipped open the buttons of his uniform jacket.

'Leo? What are you doing?' Juno murmured.

To her total astonishment, he winked at her as he took off the jacket, then draped the heavy brocade garment over her shoulders. The fabric was warm from his skin, the jacket large enough to reach her knees, enveloping her in the scent of soap and sandalwood and clean male. An older female guest nearby sighed, the hum of approval from the crowd matched by the strange glow suffusing Juno's chest at the chivalrous gesture.

'Let's go.' Leo grasped her hand and headed towards the balcony doors.

The colour rose in her cheeks as he led her through the adoring crowd. She felt like the head of the cheerleading squad, wearing the captain of the football team's letter jacket after a winning game, times about a hundred. Except she'd never been a cheerleader in high school and never been on the captain of the football team's radar.

It was a heady feeling, but also kind of shocking, not just to be singled out by Leo, but to know it could make her feel important, when she had always laughed at those girls in the past.

Leo grasped the crystal handle and pulled open the heavy glass door to the balcony, then executed a sweeping, mocking bow.

'After you, Your Majesty,' he said as the blast of cold air chilled Juno's flushed cheeks. 'Our private sanctuary awaits.'

Memories of that night eight years ago

clogged Juno's throat. She'd surprised him out here then, having snuck down from her room to catch a glimpse of her crush. She'd grown up since then, a lot, because she'd had to, hiding her mother's addictions while dealing with all the responsibilities her mother had abandoned over the years. And lost any belief in fairy tales.

But as she stepped outside, the frozen air misting her vision, a part of that wild, troubled but still innocent child stepped into the night with her. And a lump got lodged in her chest making it hard for her to breathe.

Let it go. You're not that besotted kid any more.

This wasn't romantic, she told herself staunchly. Leo had an agenda—he wanted a political union, and probably to get into her pants.

But even as her natural cynic tried to control her breathing, the lump grew, threatening to block off her air supply, as Leo stepped onto the balcony behind her. His big body shielded hers as he rested his hands on her shoulders.

The door slammed shut behind them. And suddenly she was alone with him in the still night. Her pulse accelerated to warp speed.

He pressed his face into her hair, and inhaled.

'Your new scent is killing me,' he murmured. 'It reminds me of summer. What made you change it? Because I definitely approve.'

'I wanted to torture you…' she said, pushing the words out past the ever-expanding lump—she'd started wearing this scent eight years ago to impress him with how grown up she was. It hadn't had the desired effect then.

'It worked.' The rough chuckle against her nape was a salute to that desperate teenager. 'Vanilla doesn't suit you.'

She tensed, the moment of panic not helping with her breathing difficulties. Jade had told her during their long exchange of details to be careful of Leo, that he was an exceptionally observant man.

Juno had dismissed the warning. If Leo was so observant why hadn't he been aware of her long campaign to get him to notice her that summer?

But Jade had been right. And whatever happened tonight, she couldn't afford to have their ruse exposed.

But the danger of discovery only increased her excitement as Leo gripped her hand—his fingers warm, hers already chilling—and led her away from the prying eyes of the crowd inside the ballroom, to the far end of the snowy balcony.

Towering over her, his body heat warming her, he cupped her cheek, then ran his thumb over the line of her lips. 'How did I not notice how exquisite you are until tonight?' he murmured.

Her cheeks heated, panic and exhilaration combining in the pit of her belly, as his gaze lifted to her tiara and then glided down.

Was it her sister he saw now? Or her?

She shivered.

'How are you not freezing?' she managed, trying for mocking but getting breathless instead.

He barked out a laugh. 'Great circulation,' he said, but then he framed her face in both hands and tilted her head up to the torchlight. 'And hours of anticipation.'

He lowered his mouth, his wide sensual lips hovering over hers—the tantalising promise hurtling her back in time.

'Kiss me, Princess,' he demanded.

Her mouth opened on a sob of longing and welcomed him in.

* * *

Leo threaded his fingers into the silky locks at the Queen's nape and claimed her mouth. At last.

Her lips softened, her throaty moan a siren call to his already overwrought senses. He captured the sultry taste of wine and desire, as the kick of need throbbed in his groin.

The woman had bewitched him, all evening, and the only way to break the enchantment was to give them both what they needed.

Her fingertips settled on his waist, making the muscles of his abdomen tense and the burgeoning erection throb as the kiss became carnal in a heartbeat.

He grasped her hips to draw her closer. The satin glided under his hands like a whisper, but the feel of the firm, toned body beneath, the lush curves shivering under his touch, sent the twist of need into his gut.

His tongue tangled with hers, exploiting, demanding, so hungry for the taste of her he doubted he would ever be sated. He found her nipple with his thumb, rigid beneath the thin satin of her dress; she gasped but arched towards him in an instinctive cry for more.

He drew the bodice down, ducked his head to warm the taut pebble with his lips, her scent surrounding him now. He drew her breast into his mouth, felt her buck in his arms, as her nipple engorged. The frantic need echoed in his groin. Holding her in place, he found the apex of her thighs through the gown, pressed the heel of his hand where he knew she would need it the most. He heard the tortured sob. The sudden desire to pull up her gown and find the slick nub with his fingers was so sharp and shocking, he tore his mouth away from her breast. Lifted his hand to her hips.

This was more than temptation.

Too much more.

They were on a balcony, in the snow, damn it.

He dragged a staggered breath into his lungs. Her eyes were fixed on his, glazed with arousal, but also shadowed with shock as he drew the bodice of her gown back up to hide the reddened nipple.

What the hell had just happened?

He'd planned to seduce her, to charm her into agreeing to the marriage—or at least to debating it—but this sudden, visceral connection, this stark hunger didn't seem charming or expedient.

This wasn't a seduction. It was something more. Something he did not recognise. Something he wasn't even sure he could control.

She shuddered and stepped back, out of his arms, the dazed look replaced by wariness.

'That was a mistake…' she said.

Gripping the coat, *his* coat, she wrapped it tighter around her body, the body he was suddenly far too eager to explore.

'Why?' he demanded, even though a part of him agreed with her.

The taste of her had been too real, too addictive.

The benefits of a political and financial union had been the last thing on his mind as he'd fed on her surrender.

The truth was, he was finding it hard even now not to drag her back into his arms and finish what they had started. Her flushed face, and the reddened skin on her chin from his kiss, the memory of her hard nipple engorging in a rush made the throbbing in his pants painful. But why be coy?

He wanted her and she wanted him. That

didn't have to be a bad thing. In truth it could be a very good thing.

Her gaze darted away as she sank her teeth into her bottom lip.

The pounding in his pants intensified.

Not good.

He grasped her chin. 'Answer me, Jade,' he said. 'Surely discovering there is some chemistry between us—' And wasn't that the understatement of the century? '—will make a marriage between us even more beneficial.'

And hot and wild and...

Focus, Leo.

He curbed the insistent ache. And dropped his hand, to stop himself from devouring her all over again.

Her eyes flickered with something that looked like panic.

'I'm tired. I should...' She hesitated, and it occurred to him the kiss had shocked her too, as she jerked a thumb over her shoulder. 'I need to go to bed. I'm exhausted.'

Really?

But the ball wasn't over yet. It had barely begun. And they had not even discussed the marriage.

He forced himself not to voice his impatience though. Her flushed face and wide eyes made her seem younger than she had a moment ago. The sense of déjà vu niggled at the back of his mind—why did he feel as if he had been here before with her?—but he dismissed it.

'As you wish, Jade,' he said, shoving his hands into his pockets, to control the desire to drag her back into his arms.

She was an innocent, he needed to remember that. What had just happened had shocked him as well.

'Let's continue this discussion tomorrow.' *Once we've both calmed down enough to have a conversation.*

'Yes, let's… Thank you.' Her visible relief made him smile.

She would be his, all he had to do was wait.

'I'll… I'll see you tomorrow. When do you leave?' she asked.

He frowned; didn't she know the schedule? 'Noon.'

'Okay, good,' she said, then rushed past him.

He watched her disappear around the side of the building—the sight of her in his jacket as appealing as everything else he had discovered about the woman he was now determined to make his bride.

Before tonight, all he'd seen were the political and economic benefits of their union. But tonight he had discovered that there would be considerable fringe benefits too.

The Queen was skittish, that much was obvious. But perhaps that was to be expected. Until tonight there had been no hint of any chemistry between them. Especially not a chemistry of this magnitude. The truth was the intense passion between them had blindsided him; he wanted to be able to control it, before they took this further.

But if it had blindsided him, what must it have done to her? After all, she had no experience of men.

He strolled to the balcony door, the chilly air prickling over his skin. But instead of returning to the ballroom he took the path she'd chosen around the side of the building.

The chivalrous thing to do would be to return to the ball.

But despite outward appearances he was not a chivalrous man, he was a realist. And if he did not return to the ball either, rumours would be rife tomorrow about their joint disappearance.

Rumours he could exploit.

CHAPTER THREE

JUNO AWOKE THE next morning, groggy and disorientated.

Am I dreaming?

Her brain and body struggled to adjust to the alien feel of luxury cotton sheets, and the unfamiliar sight of thick velvet drapes, antique furniture and the view through a tall mullioned window—not of the fire escape of the apartment block opposite hers, but of an enchanting Alpine vista blanketed in snow.

Then her gaze alighted on the uniform jacket draped over one of the armchairs, the memory of hot lips had her nipples drawing into tight peaks and reality came rushing back.

Monrova. Jade. The swap. The ball. *Leo.*

She pressed her fingers to her chin, where Leo's kiss had left a mark.

The man was a born kisser. That kiss had been more than worth an eight-year wait.

But the memory of what had happened next

had the heat flushing through her system again. She cupped her swollen breast, felt the molten spot between her thighs where his hand had pressed for a few terrifying seconds of bliss.

A light tap sounded on the bedroom door, jerking her out of the erotic trance.

'Your Majesty, it's Serena, I'm here with Jennifer. Are you awake?'

Serena? Jennifer? Oh, yes, her sister's personal assistant and her personal maid.

'Yes. Give me a minute,' she said, dragging her still-aching body out of her sister's bed.

She checked her sister's phone.

It was past noon. Leo and his entourage had been due to leave by noon.

A strange combination of relief and disappointment echoed through her confused body. It was for the best, she told herself staunchly— as soon as he had told her the time of his departure she had intended to avoid seeing him again at all costs.

Leo was a dangerous man. Not just observant, but demanding and so hot he had incinerated her control and her common sense last night. One kiss and she had been his, revelling in his touch, his taste, her body not her own. She couldn't afford to get that close to him again.

She tugged on a silk robe. Tied her hair back, so that neither woman noticed it was shorter than her sister's, and tried to calm her racing heartbeat. Not easy, considering she was hopelessly jet-lagged, she was still struggling with last night's kiss bombshell and, unlike Jade, she had never been a morning person.

'Come in, Serena,' she called out.

The middle-aged woman hurried into the bedroom with a harassed look on her face, followed by the younger woman who was carrying a tray loaded with...

Breakfast... *Yum.*

And coffee.

Praise the Lord.

'Your Majesty, are you well?' Serena said, clutching a bunch of the morning papers, while Jennifer proceeded to put the tray on a small table by the window and set out her breakfast. 'I have taken the precaution of making an appointment with the palace physician.'

'I'm great, Serena, no doctor needed,' Juno said, grabbing a slice of toast off the tray and slathering on some butter.

Note to self: set an alarm tomorrow.

Her sister probably got up at dawn no matter what time she'd been up the night before.

'You can cancel the appointment. Sorry I overslept. Last night was…' *What?* Intriguing? Astonishing? Terrifying? Dangerously exciting? 'Quite tiring,' she said, as she sat down in one of the room's armchairs. After finishing the toast in a few quick bites, she grabbed the coffee cup Jennifer had just finished pouring.

'Thank you, Jennifer, you're a lifesaver.' She inhaled the delicious scent before swallowing a life-saving gulp. 'Perfect.'

'Thank you, Your Majesty.' The maid curtsied. 'Would you like me to add the cream and sugar now?'

Juno plopped the cup back down on the tray. *Oops.* 'Oh, yes, of course.'

She'd totally forgotten her sister's sweet tooth.

Juno watched, dismayed, as the maid loaded the coffee with enough cream and sugar to give any normal person tooth rot. She took another sip and tried not to gag.

'Mmm, lovely, Jennifer. Thank you, that's just how I like it.'

Really, Jade?

Serena finished talking on the phone. 'I've cancelled the appointment, Your Majesty, if you're absolutely sure you're well?'

'Yes, really.' She could not risk getting examined by the palace doctor. She and Jade were identical, but she had a small scar on her knee she'd got skidding into home base aged twelve—and a unicorn on her hip.

She'd got the tattoo on her eighteenth birthday—a month after her mom's death, and the day after their Central Park apartment had been repossessed.

At the time it had been a statement of purpose. Proof that she was a survivor. Right now it would be an even bigger statement she was an imposter.

'Okay, wonderful,' Serena said, but she still looked harassed. 'His Majesty will be so pleased. Could I tell him you'll be down in twenty minutes?'

'Sorry? What?' Juno said, dumping the cup back on the tray.

Leo was still here?

Suddenly swallowing the sugary coffee without vomiting was the least of her worries. The twist of anxiety in her gut was nothing compared to the incendiary buzz of sensation firing over every inch of her body.

'I'm sorry to rush you,' Serena said. 'But he's been quite insistent. Apparently he has been speaking to Major Garland about your schedule and he wants to discuss a significant change after last night's events at the ball.'

Last night's events at the ball?

Juno's skin began to heat. The memory of Leo's lips on her breast—so firm, so forceful, so demanding—far too vivid.

The woman laid the papers she had under her arm on the breakfast table. 'The reaction to the news of your romance has been overwhelmingly positive, by the way.'

Their romance! What romance?

Juno blinked, the heat exploding in her cheeks, and several other places besides, as she scanned the newspapers—her breathing becoming increasingly difficult.

Check Mate: Has the King Finally Taken His Queen?
Is Royal Romance Confirmed at Last in Monrova?

Having a Ball, All Night Long!
Look of Love for King Leo and his Future Queen?

Each headline was illustrated with tons of candid shots… Of her and Leo looking loved up as they flirted during the banquet and danced far too close together. But the worst were the shots taken from a variety of angles as he followed her out onto the balcony, her body swamped by his coat. The anticipation on her face would have put a child who had just been given their very own candy store to shame.

No. No. No.

How had she managed to trash the reputation of Monrova's monarchy in one night?

Not that she usually gave a damn about the reputation of the monarchy, not since her father had made it clear it was more important to him than she was. But she was giving a damn about it now—because trashing the monarchy's reputation meant trashing her sister's reputation too.

She'd messed up. Again. And Jade would be the one to pay the price.

'While he has been rather impatient this morning, I suppose it is to be expected.'

Serena's words interrupted Juno's mental walk of shame. 'Excuse me?'

The woman's blush had faded, and her expression had softened. 'I should have congratulated you, Your Majesty. I really had no idea the negotiations had gone this far. But you do make such a romantic couple. I don't know why I didn't see it before. Everyone will be overjoyed when you set a date.'

Negotiations? Date? What. The. Actual...?

Juno slapped her hand on the papers. 'Right, I see,' she said, trying to think round the wodge of panic threatening to choke her.

She hadn't agreed to anything last night. Had she?

The end of the evening, after that clinch on the balcony, had been a blur, her senses still reeling from the shock of discovering Leo was a kiss ninja.

She pursed her lips, the tingle returning full force.

Stop thinking about him and start thinking about how on earth you're going to get out of this—without everyone finding out that you are not your sister.

'Your Majesty, we really must get you ready.'

Serena's beatific smile had faltered as she whipped out her phone. 'I promised His Majesty faithfully he would not have to wait too much longer to see you. He's a rather forceful man, is he not?'

Forceful? Yeah, that was one way of putting it.

She pushed the tray to one side. She'd lost her appetite anyway. She really did not want to see Leo again. He was her kryptonite, the unpredictable effect he had on her something she wasn't sure she had any control over. But from the look on Serena's face, she knew she didn't have a choice. How could she get out of this meeting without making Jade's assistant and everyone else suspicious?

'Okay, Serena,' she said. 'Could you let Leo know I'll be there as soon as I can, I promise?'

Juno headed for the shower, hoping against hope she could come up with some kind of a plan—to handle her catastrophic fall from grace last night and the rumours about their 'romance' but, most importantly of all, Leo's devastating ability to make her forget everything except the promise of pleasure.

* * *

'Her Majesty, the Queen of Monrova.'

Leo turned from his contemplation of the snowy landscape—a view he had been admiring for over an hour now—to see Queen Jade enter the room with her personal assistant.

Wearing designer jeans and a sweater, her hair tied up in a knot, she should have looked neat and pretty and demure—the same impression she'd made on him during their meeting a month ago. But as she walked towards him, his gaze snagged on the way the skinny jeans and sweater clung to her curves, and his fingers burned to free her hair from the prim topknot. It didn't suit her now, the way it had before, some tantalising tendrils already escaping from confinement to cling to the line of her neck.

How would she taste if he placed his mouth on the pulse point?

'King Leonardo, I'm so sorry to have kept you waiting so long,' she said.

King Leonardo? Not Leo?

He frowned at her strained smile as she held out her fingers in greeting. So she was going to pretend last night had never happened.

He captured her fingers in his, lifted them to his lips and watched the smile falter.

'You seem to be making a habit of it, Jade,' he said as he released her.

She brushed the back of her hand against her jeans, probably trying to ease the sensation still lingering on his lips. He smiled, glad to see she was as incapable of controlling that buzz as he was.

'I'm afraid I overslept, Your Majesty,' she said, the snap in her voice amusing him.

There she was, the spitfire from last night. Demure be damned. This woman was about as far from demure as it was possible to get. Who would have guessed he would find that so hot?

'But there was no need to delay your departure,' she added, the stubborn tilt of her chin telling him to back off. 'Your Majesty.'

Unfortunately for her, he had the upper hand here and he intended to use it. The media had happily spread the story this morning, insinuating in that adorable way they had that he and Jade had already consummated their marriage plans last night after their joint early departure from the ball. Little did they know how close they had almost come to doing just that.

No way was he backing off now.

While she had been lying in bed—he stifled the image of her lush body, naked, beneath the sheets—he had been busy devising a plan with the obsequious cooperation of Jade's chief of staff, Major Garland, who it transpired was very keen to facilitate the marriage, because it had been her father's wishes.

Leo did not like the man. Officious and opinionated and old school and happy to ride roughshod over the Queen's wishes if he thought it suited her dead father's agenda, Garland reminded Leo of his own father's advisors, men he had been quick to fire as soon as he had acceded to the throne.

Humiliation closed his throat, as the phantom pain of his father's riding crop stung his backside.

Perhaps Garland wasn't as bad as those bastards, who had turned a blind eye to his father's excessive attachment to corporal punishment, but the major was in the same mould. Right now, though, Garland's support was useful.

'Of course I delayed my departure, Jade,' he said.

She scowled at the deliberate use of her given

name and he had to bite down on his lip to stop a chuckle bursting out.

I swallowed your sobs of pleasure last night, and felt your body soften as mine hardened. Do you really believe we can pretend that never happened?

'We have much to discuss about our impending nuptials,' he finished.

Her eyebrows shot up her forehead.

'But… We haven't agreed anything,' she said, looking flustered and unsure.

She really was very different from the woman he remembered, who had been so placid, so pragmatic about discussing this topic. But they hadn't known then what they knew now. That this did not have to be simply a sterile political union.

'The press would disagree, after last night,' he said.

'But nothing happened last night,' she said as a guilty flush illuminated the freckles sprinkled across her nose.

He stifled the urge to tug her towards him and kiss each one in turn.

Focus, Leo.

'Really?' he said, raising a brow. 'Nothing

at all?' he murmured, letting his gaze drift to her breasts and enjoying her answering blush.

'Well, nothing much.' She pursed her lips into a tight line.

Yup, she was still being tortured too.

'Regardless, I believe the judicious course of action now would be to capitalise on the positive publicity from last night and take this opportunity to explore our connection.'

'Our... Our connection?' she said, her eyes widening—with horror but also awareness. And awareness he could use.

'Yes, our connection.' He took her hand, which hung limply by her side, and ran his thumb across the back of it—to soothe her nerves, while also staking his claim.

She was young. And inexperienced. Her understanding of men a lot less than her understanding of monarchy... Although even that seemed to have deserted her last night. But to be fair, it had deserted him, too.

He wanted to reassure her that he would not push her the way he had last night, but make her aware that, at the same time, theirs was a physical connection they could both enjoy.

'I've spoken to Major Garland and suggested

a state visit to Severene for the next week. All the usual protocols will be observed but it would be an excellent opportunity for you to be introduced to the Severene people and for them to meet you.'

And an even better opportunity for him to persuade her this marriage would have some excellent fringe benefits.

'But I can't.' She tugged her hand free and stuck it into the back pocket of her jeans, doing interesting things to her bust.

'Why not?' He forced his gaze back to her face.

Still focussing, Leo.

'Because I'm busy here,' she said. 'It's Christmas and I have stuff to do. Official stuff. And lots of it.'

'On the contrary, Your Majesty.' Garland stepped forward on cue. 'There is nothing in your schedule that can't be postponed or re-arranged.'

The stubborn chin was comprehensively contradicted by the flash of panic in her emerald eyes. 'Are you sure?'

'Absolutely, in fact I have taken the liberty of already making the necessary arrangements.

Given our recent discussion of the huge benefits of your political union with Severene and its King—and how much King Andreas wished this marriage to take place—I felt sure you would be very much in favour of taking advantage of this opportunity.'

'But it's Christmas,' she said, sounding exasperated as well as panicked now. 'Surely I should be here with *my* people, not Leo's.'

'You'll be back in time for Christmas,' Leo cut back in, stupidly pleased by her use of his given name again. 'Garland and I have arranged a seven-day visit culminating in the Severene Christmas Ball on December the eighteenth, at which you will be my guest of honour. You would return to Monrova the next day.'

He stemmed the twinge of regret that she wouldn't be in Severene over Christmas itself, when she would have provided an excellent distraction from the dark thoughts that always assailed him at that time of year.

'But...' she began again, clearly searching for something...*anything* to get out of this situation.

It was a good thing he had such a robust ego—her reluctance to spend a week with him something she was not making any effort to hide.

But he found her skittishness as captivating as he had last night.

Jade's reluctance could not be about the official visit. She was an expert at participating in these kinds of events, so her reluctance had to be about him, and the chemistry they shared.

He was glad their physical connection had unsettled her so much, because it had unsettled him, too.

'But I didn't agree to this.'

He stifled the sting of sympathy.

'Your Majesty,' the overbearing Garland butted in again. 'As you know, your father was keen for this match to—'

'Enough.' Leo lifted his hand, seeing the flash of something in her eyes that surprised him. Stubborn refusal, yes, but more than that... Distress. Garland's intervention was hindering his cause now, rather than helping it.

'I wish to speak to the Queen in private,' he said, giving his own advisors a nod. They left the room immediately, knowing not to contradict their King's orders. 'Leave us, Garland,' he added.

'As you wish, Your Majesty,' the major said, and finally left too, because Leo suspected he was a chauvinist as well as a self-important stickler.

'Miss…' Leo turned to Jade's personal assistant, to dismiss her too, if he could remember her surname.

'Jenkins, Serena Jenkins,' she said, then, instead of obeying his order, she turned to her Queen. 'Your Majesty, are you happy to participate in a private audience with His Majesty?'

'I… I suppose so.' Jade blinked, as if she'd been pulled from a deep well. A well that intrigued him now as much as the rest of her. Perhaps her relationship with her father had not been as comfortable as appearances suggested? 'I suppose it can't do any more damage.'

He smiled despite the tension in the room. Damn but she was refreshingly outspoken.

Jenkins curtsied and left them alone together.

The hunger that had kept him up half the night surged. No longer able to resist, he pressed his palm to the flushed skin of her cheek.

She stiffened, but didn't draw away.

'Relax, Jade,' he said. 'I'm not going to devour you,' he murmured, even though he had to admit he wanted to.

Which was not like him at all.

He enjoyed women, and he enjoyed sex. But he had never felt this visceral need before.

He let his hand drop. Disturbed by the thought.

'I don't want to go on this state tour or visit or whatever,' she said, the flash of anger in her eyes a potent partner to the arousal.

'You have made that very apparent, Your Majesty,' he said, determined not to be charmed by her candour again. They had a shared purpose, which had only been enhanced by what had happened on that balcony, and he was struggling to understand why she could not see it. 'To which I would have to ask, why? Garland is a pompous ass, but he is your advisor, and until last night you too understood the political value of our union.'

She blinked, clearly dismayed by the reprimand. He hadn't intended to be quite so blunt with her, but he'd be damned if he would allow her to ignore the huge benefits of the plan he had outlined with Garland.

'Right…okay,' she said, clearly flustered.

Turning, she walked to the window, and wrapped her arms around her waist. He could see the tension in her body, and thought he understood it. 'I just…' she murmured, her voice so low he could barely hear it. 'I just didn't want to spend a week in Severene. I was looking forward to having no official duties now until after Christmas.'

He followed her to the window, his gaze roaming over her hair as he stood behind her. He shoved his hands into his pockets, resisting the desire to place his lips on the sensitive skin of her nape and breathe in the enchanting scent that had intoxicated him the night before. Now was not the time to claim the spoils of victory—or ignite a spark he still wasn't entirely sure he could control.

He understood what her real reservations were about joining him on this tour, even if she did not. This wasn't about the burden of the official duties. Jade had always been prepared to do whatever it took to benefit her kingdom. Her reluctance to spend the week with him was to do with the strength of the physical connection they had discovered last night. It scared her, he got that. As much as he planned to use it to his advantage, at the same time he needed to reassure her that he would not ravish her, the way he almost had yesterday.

All of which meant, he would have to be patient now, if it killed him.

'I want you to come to Severene with me, Jade. To see the kingdom properly, to get a chance to meet my people and for them to meet you.'

She swung round, her gaze both wary and tense. 'Really, is that all?'

'Not quite,' he said and, before he could stop himself, he touched his thumb to the tendril of hair that had slipped from her topknot and dangled enticingly over her cheekbone. Testing the texture between his thumb and forefinger, he hooked it behind her ear. 'I enjoyed last night immensely,' he said, the husky tone as raw as the desire searing his throat.

Arousal had darkened her irises to black, something she could not hide.

He tucked his hand back into his trouser pocket.

Don't push, Leo. Not yet.

She reminded him of an unbroken colt. What she needed now was persuasion, not pressure.

'And I want a chance to take it further,' he added, gratified when her cheeks coloured. 'Much further. But I will allow you to set the pace.'

'Really?' she said.

'Yes, really,' he concurred, prepared to give her the time she needed.

'But what if I don't measure up?' she said. 'As Queen, I mean. To your people?'

He frowned. What an odd thing to say. Of course she would make a good queen. She'd been trained for the role her whole life, just as he had. And she was already doing an exemplary job with her own subjects. 'I doubt that will be a problem.'

'You don't think so? After the scandal I've already caused?' He detected the note of vulnerability he'd found so fascinating the night before.

'*We* caused,' he corrected her. 'And the results of which we both enjoyed, so I'm not going to lose sleep over it,' he said, because he had lost enough sleep already over the memory of her lips opening for him, her nipple engorging under his tongue, that soft sob of...

For goodness' sake, focus, Leo.

'Okay, I'll do it. I'm come to Severene,' she said, as if they hadn't already agreed on it. 'But if the visit is a disaster, there'll be no more talk of marriage. Okay?'

It sounded as if she thought she was striking some kind of bargain.

He nodded, deciding to humour her. 'Absolutely. Not another word on the subject,' he said.

Because he intended to ensure, at the end of those seven days, their decision to marry would be nothing more than a formality.

CHAPTER FOUR

How did I get here? And how do I get away again without messing everything up?

Juno stepped out of the private jet and stopped dead.

The barrage of flashes from the herd of press photographers held behind a cordon blinded her. The shouts and clicks became deafening.

How does Jade stand it?

'Jade, is there a problem?' Leo's steady voice interrupted her thoughts—until his palm landed on the base of her spine to direct her out of the plane and a whole new level of panic exploded along her nerve-endings.

'No, not at all,' she said, forcing herself to move.

He took her arm to lead her down the steps to a series of dignitaries lined up on the tarmac. She shook their hands, her mind dazed and her body far too aware of Leo's nearness.

Since he'd pressed her into going on this trip

approximately five hours ago, he'd ignored her, while she'd been bombarded with instructions and information from her staff. But she'd taken barely any of it in, because she'd been completely unable to ignore him in return.

He'd greeted her at the airport and then spent the forty-minute flight over the mountains being briefed by his advisors while she was going over the schedule of events that had been arranged for her in Severene with Serena.

What the heck did she know about how to conduct herself during a walkabout of Severene's old town or a carol concert in the cathedral or the state opening of the capital's famous Christmas market? She wasn't a queen. She was a fraud.

But as Leo did the introductions, keeping her close by his side, her concern over all the things she did not know about her new role was nothing compared to the major pheromone freak-out going on because his big body and that tantalising scent were totally invading her personal space.

Having introduced her to the last of the dignitaries—all of whose names she instantly forgot—Leo directed her to the waiting limousine.

A uniformed chauffeur bowed and opened the door.

She stopped, Leo's hand still causing havoc on her back.

The dark leather interior looked warm and intimate. Way too intimate.

'Shouldn't I travel with Serena?' she managed to ask, glancing back to see her PA standing several yards away with the other advisors. 'I've still got a ton of work to do on the schedule briefing,' she added. It wasn't even a lie; she had no clue what she was doing over the next week.

Leo's dark brow lifted. 'You'll have time for that this evening. The first item on the agenda was our sleigh procession through the old town to the palace—the crowds are already assembled.'

They were?

She hadn't noticed that item on the agenda, but then she'd been too busy trying to ignore Leo and the effect he had on her to notice much of anything.

'Then why are we getting in a limo?' she asked, still delaying.

His hand shifted on her back, sending the

shivers into overdrive. 'To drive to the barracks where the procession is ready for us. Are you scared to be alone with me, Jade?'

Absolutely.

'Of course not,' she lied, trying to sound outraged despite the heat in her cheeks.

His lips quirked at her indignant reply. She wasn't fooling him any more than she was fooling herself.

'Then get in the car, Your Majesty,' he demanded, calling her bluff.

Left with no choice, she scooted into the limo.

The leather interior only became more intimate as he joined her. They were several feet apart on either side of the large car, but even so she was too aware of him as the chauffeur sealed them in together.

Her pulse beat harder as the car drove off, winding down the Alpine gorge through the forest. She stared out of the window. She had to find a strategy for dealing with her reaction to Leo.

'While I find it remarkably flattering,' he began as she tried to concentrate on the incredible scenery outside the car, instead of inside it, 'there is no need to be quite so jumpy when you are alone with me. I promise not to touch you again... Unless you ask me.'

'It's not that...' *It so is that.* 'I'm just not sure we should present ourselves as a couple. I don't want everyone to be disappointed when the marriage doesn't happen.'

Leo's rough chuckle sent the shivers straight back up her spine. 'They won't be,' he murmured... And she heard the words he hadn't said.

Because the marriage will happen.

'But you can also rest assured you won't be required to do more than you would normally do on these occasions,' he added.

She turned, to find him watching her.

The panic sprinted up her spine to join the inappropriate shivers.

Leo is an exceptionally observant man.

'Right, great,' she said as her sister's warning echoed in her ears.

Relax, Ju, or you'll blow your cover.

Stressing about what she didn't know about being a queen—which was pretty much everything—was the least of her worries. The truth was making a bad impression on this trip might not be a bad thing. It might be the only way to put Leo off the prospect of their 'political union with benefits'.

Being herself—without giving away her real identity—shouldn't even be that hard, because she'd effectively been doing it for four years, while building her social-media profile as the Rebel Princess.

She'd created the illusion of being a princess in exile—pampered and privileged and yet streetwise enough to connect with the general public—without ever letting on how tough her life had been. Aspirational was good on social media, micro celebrity even better; a homeless eighteen-year-old with debts she couldn't pay and a mother who had died of chronic alcohol abuse, not so much.

Her social-media activity had been a lifesaver after her mom's death. She'd bartered her Rebel Princess brand, such as it was, into enough of a money-spinner to keep herself afloat with the help of several dead-end jobs, without ever having to ask her father for a handout. But she'd been only too happy to jettison it a month ago when she'd been recruited to head up Byrne IT's Social Media Engagement Team. She'd come to hate the fakeness of everything she posted as the Rebel Princess. But her ability to project an image, play a role, would come in handy now. All she had to do was be convincing as the Queen of Monrova while also turning Leo off the idea of marriage.

The limousine pulled into the gates of an army barracks and stopped in front of a parade of uniformed horsemen—resplendent in the red and gold colours of Severene's national flag—and an ornate sledge complete with a team of six white stallions.

She swallowed. The chauffeur opened her door and she stepped out.

The dusky light shone off the snowy landscape and she could see the palace of Severene, tall and majestic, perched above the old town in the distance.

Leo got out of the other side of the car and walked round to offer her his arm.

'Your Majesty, your carriage awaits,' he said, the mocking tone almost as captivating as the sizzles of sensation that leapt up her arm and sank deep into her belly.

She had to play the role of Queen—enough to be convincing, but no more than that.

But as Leo escorted her to the carriage, the

uniformed cavalry all saluting him as they passed, she knew not having her cover blown wasn't her biggest challenge.

Resisting Leo and avoiding a repeat of what had happened on the balcony was going to be the much bigger ask.

'Ready?' he asked, after they had settled in their seats in the sleigh, a fur rug covering their knees.

As I'll ever be.

'Smile, Jade, and relax, they love you already,' Leo murmured to his travelling companion as the royal sledge passed the crowds of spectators lining the route through Severene's old town towards the palace. The crowd were cheering, excited to see the woman they were keen to believe might become their new Queen.

He knew how they felt.

He turned to the crowd, threw a salute or two as they passed through the old town's central plaza and the sledge glided over cobbled streets buried under a layer of snow.

He noticed that Jade directed her attention to specific people in the crowd. The crowd clearly enjoyed the personal connection, but he wondered why her father's courtiers hadn't taught her the best way to conserve her energy? Exerting too much effort when waving could give you arm-ache.

She waved enthusiastically at a small boy being held on his father's shoulders. She swung round as they left the child and his father behind, her eyes sparkling with exhilaration.

'Did you see that little boy?' she said. 'I think he was waving at you.'

'Doubtful,' he said, surprised by her enthusiasm. 'You're enjoying yourself?'

'Actually, I am. It's exhilarating, isn't it?'

Is it?

Seriously? What was so exciting about a royal procession? Hadn't she done a million of these before?

He'd never found this part of the job appealing. 'I told you, they love you already,' he said, willing to use the evidence to his advantage.

'They don't love me, they don't know me,' she said, looking momentarily surprised by the idea. 'But they obviously love you.'

He frowned, taken aback by the observation. Was she mocking him?

'They don't love me,' he said. 'That's not my role.'

The one thing he could congratulate his father on was that he had always ensured the Kings of the Royal House of Severo were respected, not loved. Maintaining distance and dignity with people you had been born to rule was important. Maintaining your privacy even more so. Or this circus could consume your life.

She watched him, her scrutiny making him uncomfortable. 'Then whose role is it?'

'The Queen's,' he murmured, but even as he said it, the brutal spike of memory—from another Christmas, a long time ago—made a strange band tighten around his chest.

'Why don't you join the other children, Leo? I'm sure Santa has a present for you too.'

'Papa said I must not. That my job is by your side, Mama.'

'Papa isn't always right, my sweet boy.'

'Why is it only the Queen's role? Isn't that a bit sexist?' Jade said, pulling him out of the uncomfortable memory.

He preferred not to remember his mother, especially at this time of year.

He smiled, amused by how direct she was. 'You disapprove?'

She stared at him. 'Of course, if they can love your Queen, why can't they love you too?'

'Perhaps that's the way I prefer it,' he said, noting her reference to 'your Queen'—as if that Queen was not going to be her.

He had work to do. Then again, he had always enjoyed a challenge.

'Why would you prefer them not to love you?' she asked.

'Because I'm not a sentimental man,' he answered honestly. 'And love isn't something I require.'

It was her turn to frown. 'Doesn't everyone need love?' she asked.

The statement was so guileless, it wrongfooted him for a moment.

Should he lie? And give her some appropriate platitude? After all, he was trying to woo her into marriage. But if she agreed to this marriage, he reasoned, she needed to be aware of the limitations. He certainly did not want her to believe their union could go beyond the physical and the political.

'Not everyone needs love, no,' he said. 'Some

of us are self-sufficient and don't require that kind of connection. And emotional self-sufficiency is an invaluable commodity in a monarch, wouldn't you agree?'

Surely her own parents' marriage and the scandalous way it had collapsed was proof of that.

Her father, King Andreas, had made as much clear to Leo all those years ago, the summer he had been in Monrova on a trade mission, just after he had acceded to the throne of Severene. That was the summer the King's unruly younger daughter had developed a crush on him, and Andreas had first suggested a marriage to Jade.

At the time, his older daughter and heir had only been sixteen though, and Leo had baulked at the suggestion. He was not a cradle snatcher.

And in truth, the younger twin was the only one of Andreas's daughters he'd noticed that summer, probably because she had been so persistent in trying to get his attention.

But Leo still remembered the conversation he'd had with King Andreas the evening after the younger girl had tried to kiss him. He hadn't mentioned the incident to her father, but he had wondered if the man had discovered the truth somehow, because he had made a point of warning Leo off any entanglement with Princess Juno. At the time, Leo had found the suggestion amusing.

But he could still remember Andreas's candid words of warning because it had spoken volumes about the failure of the man's marriage.

'Juno is undisciplined and reckless and she always has been. She lacks the temperament for monarchy and since she has been living in New York I'm afraid she has become as much of a problem as her mother. Take it from me, Leonardo, pick your Queen with care and with a level head. Infatuation is never a good basis under which to make those crucial decisions. I speak from bitter experience.'

It was all Andreas had said on the subject that night, but Leo knew the story of his ill-fated marriage to Alice Monroe—the beautiful young actress Andreas had met at a UN reception in New York and then married less than a month later. Alice was a media darling and their whirlwind romance and fairy-tale wedding had captivated the press the world over. But not long after their twin daughters had arrived almost exactly nine months later, the cracks had begun to show.

By the time Andreas had finally divorced his Queen eight years later and sent her packing back to New York with their younger daughter, Alice's increasingly scandalous behaviour had come close to bringing down the Monrovan monarchy, and Leo was not surprised the man had regretted that initial infatuation.

Jade, his heir, had been the only good thing to come from it.

'Do you really believe that being royal means you don't need to be loved?' Jade asked, incredulous.

'That's not what I said,' he murmured, even though it was what he believed. 'But I do believe it can be an inconvenience that is better avoided.'

Her frown was replaced by something that looked disturbingly like pity. 'I see,' she said and looked away.

He stiffened, annoyed. Was it *him* she pitied? Why? Surely she of all people must know that love—or rather infatuation, for that was the emotion people often mistook for love—had no place in a royal marriage?

The sledge glided into the palace courtyard where a line of dignitaries and the palace's two-hundred-strong household staff waited to greet their arrival.

A young footman in the palace livery approached and opened the sled door, then unfolded the step. Bowing his head as was customary, he raised his hand to help Jade alight.

Taking his offered assistance, she bounced down from the carriage. But then to Leo's utter astonishment, she turned her attention on the young man.

'Hi, and thank you,' she said.

The footman blushed, glancing up from his bowed position, not used to being addressed directly.

'Your Highness,' the young man murmured, bowing so low Leo was surprised he didn't topple over. 'We are so honoured to have you in Severene.'

'And I'm honoured to be here,' she said. 'What's your name?'

'It's...' The young man's gaze connected with Leo's, the flush on his cheeks turning scarlet.

Leo nodded as he climbed down from the

carriage behind Jade, giving the boy permission to speak to the Queen.

'It's Klaus, Your Majesty,' the footman said, looking completely nonplussed, but as he bowed again he shivered visibly.

'It's lovely to meet you, Klaus,' Jade murmured. 'Can I ask you how long you've been standing out in the cold?'

'About an hour, Your Majesty.'

'You're not serious, in that outfit?'

The boy nodded. And the Queen of Monrova turned, her gaze fierce as it connected with Leo's.

'Leo, this is ridiculous. Look what he's wearing. He hasn't even got proper gloves on,' she said.

'Yes, I see your point,' he said. She was right. The staff uniforms, although ornate, were hardly substantial enough for sub-zero temperatures. But it was the passion flashing in her eyes that fascinated him. Even though it was a cliché he had never subscribed to, he had to admit the Queen was quite breathtaking when she was mad.

'Who's in charge here?' she demanded.

'I suppose that would be me,' Leo said,

even though strictly speaking it was the palace's Head of Household, Pierre La Clerk, who would have made the decision to have the staff stand outside. But he preferred to have all her passion directed at him.

An urge so perverse he would have to examine it later.

'Then don't just stand there, Leo,' she snapped. 'We have to get these people indoors immediately.'

He should have been outraged, of course. No one spoke to him like that and no one gave him orders. But instead he was captivated. Her unconventional approach—and her passionate determination to protect the young man shivering in his uniform—making him realise what a formidable queen she would make him.

Nodding, he clicked his fingers. And called over his head of household as another thought occurred to him.

Would he even have noticed the boy's discomfort? Highly unlikely, he realised. Ever since he could remember, state visitors were greeted in this way. Why had he never considered changing this arrangement before now?

Le Clerk approached with a stiff smile on his

face—telegraphing his disapproval at the delay. Leo didn't care. The man had made a mistake.

'Your Majesty, if there is a problem with the—' Pierre began.

'Pierre, move the introductions indoors,' Leo interrupted him. 'Klaus here is freezing and no doubt so are the rest of the staff.'

'But, Your Majesty, it is tradition for—'

'Tradition be damned if it is going to give the staff frostbite.'

Pierre's lips pursed, but he bowed low. 'Absolutely, as Your Majesty wishes.'

Pierre, the palace butlers and the other senior staff members set about moving the welcoming committee indoors.

'Come on, Klaus, I think you probably need a hot toddy,' Jade murmured as she smiled at the young footman. 'I know I do.'

Leo watched the boy smile back at her—the worship in his eyes unmistakeable.

To think he'd once thought her reserve and her dignity were her main assets as a wife and a queen. Her unconventional style of leadership—which he hadn't even realised existed until last night at the ball—was surprisingly appealing.

The footman nodded, clearly shocked by the Queen's familiarity—weren't they all?

Leo placed his palm on the small of Jade's back—the desire to touch her undeniable.

She shuddered beneath his touch as he guided her into the palace. The electric energy that had been so provocative the night before arched between them again.

Once they had repaired to the palace's cathedral-like reception room, Leo whispered in her ear. 'Can I have a private word, Your Majesty?'

She glanced at him—and he could see the wariness in her expression, but also the heat. The recollection of her mouth hot and eager on his fired through his system.

His palm remained on the small of her back as he directed her towards his private study. Getting her alone again might not be the wisest plan, but he'd be damned if he wasn't going to press his suit every chance he got.

Here it comes.

'Why did you want to see me alone?' Juno stepped away from Leo as soon as they entered his study, hating the defensiveness in her tone.

And the strange sense of loss when he lifted his guiding hand from her back.

She'd been expecting the reprimand as soon as she had acted on instinct and demanded the introductions be moved indoors. But he'd lulled her into a false sense of security. To her astonishment Leo had agreed with her in public. Even gone so far as to make arrangements immediately with his staff. But she had seen his surprise at her actions. And that should have been a massive clue—that he was simply waiting for a more private moment to let her have it.

She waited for the axe to fall. But he simply stared at her, then said: 'Why are you so defensive, Jade?'

Juno's anxiety increased. A part of her knew she had to be more subservient—or he might figure out the truth about her identity. But another part of her knew she had not been wrong to protect his footman.

Surely Jade would have done the same, although probably more diplomatically. But the result would have been the same.

'I know what you're thinking,' she said, seeing the inscrutable twist of his lips.

Was he trying to torture her, to make her

more acquiescent? Was this some kind of regal power play? Or was he trying to soften the blow because he still wanted to persuade her to agree to the marriage.

The knot in her belly tightened.

Not knowing what the heck he was thinking only made this worse.

She should never have agreed to come. Because her clever plan—to persuade him she would make him a terrible queen by being herself—was already working... But she'd just discovered it had one massive flaw.

She knew who she was. Even if Leo didn't.

So when she screwed up—either by accident or design—and Leo reprimanded her, it would be like dealing with her father all over again.

It would be a replay of all those shattering blows to her ego, and her heart, she had endured as a child, when he had looked at her with cold, disapproving eyes and told her—in actions as well as words—that she could never be royal, could never be as important as her sister, could never be worthy of his love. Dating right back to that day when she was sixteen and he had kicked her out of his life for good. She'd spent her life since that day convincing herself her father's disapproval didn't matter, that it could only hurt her if she let it matter. And now she was going to be forced to relive it. For seven days straight. When she was found wanting by a man whose opinion shouldn't matter either... But somehow it did. And she didn't even know why it did.

The anxiety began to strangle her. This whole situation was so super messed up.

Propping his butt against the desk, Leo folded his arms over his broad chest, his eyebrow lifting in challenge. 'You know what I'm thinking? Why don't you tell me what that is, then?'

Leo's disapproval did not matter. She wasn't trying to impress him. In fact the opposite was true, she was trying to persuade him she'd make him a terrible wife. And a disastrous queen.

But somehow that goal had got lost in the surge of longing that had swamped her when he had supported her decision in the courtyard. And she'd wanted to believe he really did think she'd done a good thing.

'You're going to tell me I shouldn't have been so outspoken about Klaus,' she said, because she just wanted the axe to fall now so she could deal with it. 'I know you think I should have found another, more discreet way to suggest the introductions be done indoors. That there's a right way and a wrong way to do these things and I chose the wrong way.' How many times had her father told her the same? And okay, she got it, she was not a natural at this stuff. But she was right to have done what she did. If it meant no one froze to death just to observe protocol, so be it.

'Klaus was freezing, Leo. And I refuse to apologise for making that call.'

'I see,' he said.

She braced herself for the tirade of indignation, the anger at her recklessness. The tedious lecture about her overstepping her authority and letting her emotions rule her judgement.

She should have seen this coming much sooner. Why hadn't she? As soon as he had told her during their sledge ride he didn't think emotional connections were necessary in a royal marriage, that... How had he put it? That...

'Emotional self-sufficiency is an invaluable commodity in a monarch, wouldn't you agree?'

She'd actually felt sorry for him at the time. Why would anyone believe something so sad? Sure, love could be messy and difficult and it didn't always solve everything, in fact sometimes it solved nothing at all. She'd loved her mom and she knew, in her own screwed-up way, her mother had loved her. But that love had never been enough to stop Alice Monroe loving the bottle more...

But even with all its imperfections, love was still important. It could help and it could heal. Seeing Jade again and wanting to do this swap for her sister's sake as well as her own had proved that much. And she refused to believe that anyone could survive without needing love.

Unless they were a man as cold and unfeeling as her father.

That had been her mistake. To feel sorry for Leo because she'd somehow convinced herself he wasn't that guy. When actually he was.

After all, he wanted to marry her sister to give his country a political advantage and to have a shared heir. Any man who could even contemplate something so bloodless had to be seriously messed up—no matter how much her body might desire him.

'You know, Jade,' Leo said, tilting his head to one side now as if he were studying something particularly fascinating, 'I really do not know what to make of you. And, much to my absolute astonishment, because I usually prefer predictability, I'm finding that aspect of you even more irresistible than the memory of what happened yesterday night.'

What?

Juno barely had a chance to register her shock before he had pushed off the desk, unfolded his arms and crossed the room.

She took another step back, but couldn't control the swell of relief. Or was it longing? At the dark passion in his eyes.

He cupped her cheek, the soft brush of his palm making the tangle of raw nerves in her belly unwind in a rush.

'You're not angry with me?' she heard herself say.

'Angry? Not at all,' he said, and the inscrutable smile became a genuine smile. Her heart expanded. 'You did the right thing, Jade.'

The words seemed to reach inside and touch the heart of the child she'd been, all those years ago, when her father had chastised and rejected her.

'You really think so?' she said, immediately

realising how needy she sounded when he gave a rough chuckle.

'Yes, I'm not quite the bastard you seem to think I am,' he said. 'The boy was freezing and if we'd waited much longer he might well have become hypothermic. I hate to think what the press would have made of that. And how much it would have cost the palace if he had sued.'

He was making light of the incident. But even so she could hear the respect and admiration in his tone.

He caressed her cheek. His thumb drifting across her lips.

'You should trust your instincts more,' he said, as if it were the easiest thing to do in the world. 'I don't know why you're insecure about your abilities, but, just in case no one else has ever told you this, you are an exceptionally good queen.'

She wasn't an exceptionally good queen, she wasn't any kind of a queen. But she found herself leaning into the caress anyway. And letting the joy at his heartfelt comment wrap around her heart.

His praise shouldn't mean this much to her, objectively she knew that. She didn't want it to mean this much. But subjectively, she couldn't stop herself from indulging that rejected child.

But then the needs of the woman came from nowhere. She pressed her palms to his broad chest, felt his pecs tense beneath his uniform.

His heart was beating in strong, steady punches. Her desire rose like a phoenix from the flames, making her want him so much it was almost painful.

He swore softly, then threaded his fingers into her hair and drew her face close to his. His mouth hovered over hers, tantalising, tempting, torturous.

'Ask me,' he demanded.

And so she did. 'Kiss me.'

His mouth slanted across hers, capturing her tortured gasp. Their lips locked in a battle of dominance and submission. She opened for him, losing the war. The need became painful as it throbbed between her thighs. He clasped her head in his hands, holding her in place as he devoured each sob, each sigh, each groan.

The kiss was firm, seeking, commanding, but beneath the hunger was something more. Something both brutal and tender.

She needed this; she needed him. His praise, his validation, his acceptance.

She grasped his waist, wanting more, and he groaned.

Passion shivered through her, hardening her nipples and making her body soften, the pounding in her sex so hard now it hurt.

That she could make him ache, the way she ached, that she could make him want her, so much, strengthened the surge of vindication. The surge of triumph.

But then his calloused palms slipped under the hem of the cashmere sweater she wore, and his thumbs traced the line of her waistband igniting the skin across her back. And he bit softly into her bottom lip.

The light nip was like a bomb, detonating in her sex.

She wrenched herself free and stumbled back, coming up short when she hit a leather armchair.

Her ragged breaths matched his as they stared at each other.

She touched her fingers to her lip, aware of the sting from his teeth.

He looked devastatingly gorgeous, with his

chest heaving, his dark hair mussed, the dimple in his chin even more lickable than usual and the thick ridge in his pants prominent enough to make her mouth water.

'We shouldn't have done that,' she managed on a raw gasp.

I'm not the woman you think I am.

'But we did.' He ran his tongue over his lips. Could he still taste her? Because she could taste him.

She brushed her hand through her hair and became aware that the elaborate chignon the stylist had insisted on that morning had escaped its moorings.

'We should…' She attempted to repair the damage herself, frantically repinning the unruly locks as she spoke. 'We should return to the reception, before anyone notices we're gone, and gets suspicious.'

'Everyone will have noticed by now,' he said, the wry twist of his lips impossibly hot. 'And I hate to tell you this, but I think the speculation about our relationship is a horse that bolted out of the paddock yesterday evening.' He glanced down pointedly at the evidence of his arousal. 'And is now doing a victory lap in my pants.'

The rush of heat and adrenaline racing through her body made it hard for her to concentrate. And a smile at the outrageous comment lifted her lips before she could stop it.

He huffed out a strained laugh. 'I'm glad you find my discomfort so amusing.'

'I don't, I just…' She tried to regulate her breathing, the flirtatious comment making her aware of the danger again. This was not funny, at all. He wanted to get her into compromising positions. Why had she let him? 'It's just, it's complicated…'

So *so* complicated and getting more complicated by the second.

Having Leo want her wasn't exciting. Or wonderful. Or cool. That was her sixteen-year-old self talking. It was a disaster.

Giving in to this…this explosive chemistry… would be wrong. Both ethically and emotionally and every which way in between. She wasn't the woman he thought she was, but even if she were, the kind of marriage he was suggesting was a cold, clinical abomination of the term.

Nobody should be prepared to marry for the sake of securing a political union between two countries, or to provide an heir. It was nuts.

And she was here to make him realise that, while her sister discovered the same while getting a life in New York. She was not here to obsess about his lips, or his chin dimple, or his delicious smile, or that magnificent…

Look away from his pants!

He was watching her again in that inscrutable and unbearably hot way he had, the twist of his lips more than amusement now. There was heat there too, and calculation. As if he knew exactly what her body craved and was figuring out the best way to use it against her.

Her pulse spiked.

She finished pinning up her hair as best she could and rubbed her finger across her lips hoping that her lipstick wasn't too smeared.

'Why don't I go back in first, then you can follow when…?' She glanced at the prominent ridge again that hadn't softened at all.

'You can follow when you're ready.' She made a beeline for the study door.

But as she passed him, he caught her wrist and drew her to a halt.

'Not so fast.' His thumb pressed into her pulse point, which went haywire as he tugged her round to face him. 'I want this marriage to happen. I think it will be hugely…' he paused, his eyes darkening with arousal '…beneficial for us both. And I'm not averse to persuading you how beneficial by whatever means necessary.'

It was a warning, plain and simple. She needed to be careful. To keep her hormones and everything else in check, or she might well end up doing something reckless and unforgivable… And Jade would be the one to pay the price.

Leo was a dangerous man. Arrogant, entitled, super goal-orientated and unbelievably hot. He'd already proved what a devastating effect he could have on her libido, and her best intentions, not to mention her self-control. He was a man who got what he set his sights on… And she was now in the firing line.

She dragged her hand free of his grip, rubbed her wrist where his touch had burned. 'Point taken,' she said, as haughtily as she could while her insides were giddy with a disturbing combo of nerves and guilt and…anticipation. 'But don't worry, I won't ask you to kiss me again.'

She headed for the door, ignoring the ripple of sensation that travelled up her spine from his mocking laugh. She had been warned, and she had to do everything in her power now to resist Leo, not just physically, but emotionally too.

CHAPTER FIVE

'WAIT, LEO, THERE'S a little girl over there we missed.'

Leo glanced round as Jade touched his arm, to see a small child in the thousand-strong crowd who had turned out to greet them at the opening of the Christmas market in Severene's old town. The little girl was huddled behind her mother's skirts, clutching a bunch of wilting hothouse flowers.

'You go ahead,' he murmured, surprised again by the Queen's innate ability to spot spectators who didn't push themselves forward—even if they were only two feet tall. It was a particularly impressive feat given how much the crowds had swelled in the last four days—ever since Jade's fierce defence of his freezing footman had been broadcast over the local media.

'She's your subject, Leo,' she said as she

grasped his hand. 'Why don't we go and talk to her together?'

It wasn't the first time she'd suggested such a thing. She seemed to be on a mission to break down the barriers he had always had around his interactions with Severene's population. He suspected it originated in the conversation they'd had in the sledge on her arrival, right before Freezing Footman Gate. She was testing him to see if he would buckle.

He should have found her behaviour infuriating. The request to familiarise himself with his subjects went against every tenet of his monarchy. He simply was not a people pleaser—unlike Jade—and he was not required to be. The monarchy in Severene did not rely on a sovereign grant, so there had never been any need to schmooze the public. All that was required of the royal family was that they be visible.

He also suspected this was a distraction technique. An attempt to ignore the heat that had only grown between them since she had arrived in Severene.

The more he attempted to command her attention, the more she managed to deflect or frustrate him. And it was starting to drive him more than a little insane.

Had any woman ever been so damn evasive when he was attempting to pursue her? Especially when he knew the passion between them was entirely mutual. She might be managing to resist his attempts to seduce her, but she couldn't hide the shivers of response every time he settled his hand on her back, or kissed her knuckles in public. The only problem was he had a sneaking suspicion those PDAs were tying his libido in knots, more than hers.

'To hell with it,' he murmured under his breath. 'Let's get this over with, then.'

He could see his capitulation had surprised her—the truth was he'd surprised himself. He would never normally single out individuals the way she was so adept at doing. And he found conversing with children particularly problematic, especially shy children. He didn't mean to be intimidating, but somehow he was. During these past four days, though, he'd watched Jade build an easy rapport with the people of Severene—*his* people. So really, how hard could it be?

'Are you sure?' she said, and he had to stifle a smile.

However awkward this was going to be, it would be worth it to have finally wrong-footed her for the first time in four days.

'Absolutely,' he replied, with a fervour he didn't really feel, but was more than prepared to fake.

She nodded. But then to his surprise, she smiled. An artless smile, devoid of her usual wariness. What he saw in her expression stole his breath in a way that made no sense. Because her green eyes were shadowed with something that looked very much like approval… And he didn't require anyone's approval.

They reached the line of people pressing against the ropes, and his breathing became uneven, something tugging at his memory that he knew he needed to resist.

The little girl pressed closer to her mother's side as they approached. But Jade squatted down on her haunches—not easy in the pencil skirt and heeled boots she had worn for the walkabout—so that she could converse with the child eye to eye.

'Hello, are those for me?' she asked, indicating the wilting flowers.

The small child nodded, her thumb now stuck resolutely in her mouth—was she trying to suck off her thumbnail?

'They're beautiful,' Jade said, the genuine warmth in her voice doing even stranger things to Leo's breathing, especially as he watched the child's eyes brighten.

The little girl thrust the bunch out.

'Thank you, so much,' Jade said, accepting the offering as if she'd been given a crate full of priceless jewels. How did she do that? How did she sound as if she cared when this had to be the fifth bunch of flowers she had been offered already today—and these were easily the most bedraggled?

'I'd love to know your name, so I can thank you properly,' she said, lowering her voice, ensuring that the child knew she had all her attention.

He found his own anticipation mounting, the pressure in his chest increasing, as the child considered the request and then popped her thumb out of her mouth.

'Ella,' she whispered, before stuffing her thumb back.

Jade laughed, the joyous delight in the sound making the pulse of anticipation in his chest turn to something sharp and unbidden. He tensed, shocked by his undisciplined, instinctive response.

What was wrong with him? Why was his reaction to Jade still so volatile?

'Ella? What a beautiful name,' Jade said. 'Thank you so much for these, I will treasure them.'

As she rose back to her feet, the child's mother curtsied. 'Thank you so much, Your Majesty. Ella picked them herself this morning—she was desperate to meet you after seeing you on the television. I know this means a lot to her,' the woman said, the moisture in her eyes making Leo feel uncomfortable.

How many of these walkabouts had he done in the past, without connecting with anyone? He'd always been taught to maintain a formal distance. But Jade's approach seemed so effortless, so enchanting, so...

He frowned.

He was supposed to be the one in control of

this seduction. Not her. He had planned to exploit their physical desire for one another, nothing more.

But from that first day, when Jade had rescued Klaus the palace footman from frostbite—hell, that first night, when he had placed his jacket over her shoulders and seen her eyes go a little misty—he was becoming captivated by every unpredictable move. And all the qualities in her he was discovering.

'It means a lot to me too,' Jade said graciously to the mother. 'You have a lovely child.'

The uncomfortable sensation spread under Leo's ribs. Warmth yes, admiration yes, but more than that, a disturbing feeling of connection.

And a question that he had begun to ask himself rose to the surface again.

Why did he want to marry this woman? Because the reasons that had been so simple before he had seen her again at the Winter Ball didn't seem so simple any more.

All the reasons why their union would be a good one—politically and economically for both their monarchies—still applied. In fact they had been exponentially enhanced by her visit. But beneath the expediencies was the yearning—for something that went beyond those reasons. And that disturbed him.

No woman had ever fascinated and excited him the way she did. And he knew his desire to see her each morning at their breakfast table for their schedule briefings, and his reluctance to bid her goodnight at the entrance to her suite of rooms after their evening meal, weren't just to do with his campaign to get her to agree to the marriage.

'Leo, say hello,' Jade prompted, sliding her hand into his.

The mother beamed—it had been duly noted in the press on several occasions already how romantic the people found Jade's use of the nickname. But as he heard a barrage of camera clicks, he recoiled at the thought that their observers might have seen more in his expression than he wanted them to see. More than he wanted to feel.

He bowed to the child's mother.

Do the job and then you can leave.

'A pleasure, *madame*,' he said to the mother, who curtsied and then blushed. But as he prepared to leave, the niceties handled, Jade tightened her grip on his hand.

'Didn't you forget someone?' she said. She slanted her gaze to the little girl. 'I'm sure Ella would like to say hello to you too, Leo.'

There were more clicks, and flashes and the whir of cameras—and for a hideous moment he hesitated, trapped in the glare of the spotlight. A spotlight he had become accustomed to over the years, but had always been careful to keep at a distance.

He stood frozen, the memory that had prickled at his consciousness exploding in his mind's eye.

The brutal winter wind, the sombre wail of a trumpet dirge, his father's hand gripping his hard enough to hurt, the pain in his throat as he struggled to swallow the tears.

'Your mother is dead, Leonardo. Now stop simpering. It is your job as a prince to maintain your dignity at all times.'

'Leo, is everything okay?' Jade's gentle voice dragged him free of the prison of memory.

Everyone was staring at him. The child, her mother, Jade and the press, many of whom were still firing off their shots.

'Yes, yes, of course,' he said, wanting it to be so, humiliated beyond belief.

Where the hell had that come from? And why? His mother's death had been a lifetime ago. So long ago he hardly even remembered her.

'Are you sad?' He heard a small voice and looked down to see the child staring up at him with patient, perceptive eyes. And for one weird moment, it was almost as if she could see into his soul. Or rather the soul of that little boy, who had been cast adrift in a sea of other people's tears, looking for the one face who could rescue him—only to discover she was lost for ever.

'Not any more,' he said, his voice rough with emotions he didn't want to feel—fear, panic, loneliness—but didn't seem able to stop.

The child nodded, with a gravity beyond her years, then she smiled, a sweet, innocent, inquisitive smile devoid of judgement.

'Do you love Queen Jade like me?' she asked, adoration shining in her eyes.

I hope not.

The answer sprang from nowhere, rattling him almost as much as the cruel slap of memory.

'Ella, you mustn't ask questions like that,' her mother interrupted. 'It isn't polite.'

'Have a good Christmas,' he murmured to the child, and her mother, then, grasping Jade's hand, he led her to the waiting carriage, cutting the walkabout short.

He had to escape... The crowd. The press. The scrutiny. The messy emotions he didn't want to feel. The need he did not want to acknowledge. And the miserable memory of that day, which he thought he'd buried a lifetime ago—along with his mother.

'Leo, what's wrong? What happened back there?' Juno asked, staring at the King of Severene's rigid features as the limousine drove off towards the palace.

'Nothing.' He glanced her way, then stared back out of the window, the muscle in his jaw clenched so tight it was twitching.

This was not nothing. Even though he had the outward appearance of control, this was Leo freaking out.

'The walkabout wasn't finished,' she said. Since when did Leo not stick rigidly to the schedule?

'It was getting cold,' he said, by way of explanation for the sudden change of plans.

But he didn't meet her gaze, and she knew he was lying. Something had seriously spooked him.

And that was her MO, not his.

Or it had been four days ago, until she'd begun to find her niche as the fake Queen of Monrova.

Maybe she would never be as good as Jade at this stuff. But she'd found—much to her astonishment—that she wasn't completely horrendous at it either. As they'd been ferried around a series of events and engagements in the last four days, she had discovered she enjoyed meeting the citizens of Severene. Of course, it didn't hurt that they were all so eager to meet her. That had thrown her at first, because she knew she wasn't the person they thought they were meeting. But she'd dealt with the guilt by deciding she was Jade's stand-in, doing a job that Jade couldn't do because she was busy discovering herself in New York.

Perhaps it was dishonest, but it wasn't hurting anyone. Especially if she did a decent enough job. And the numerous formal engagements had also been a brilliant way to keep her desire for Leo at bay.

So she'd thrown herself into the events, and made a real effort to win over the people she met, so as not to disgrace her sister—while at the same time keeping Severene's King and his delusions about a marriage of convenience between them at arm's length.

The only problem was that as she threw herself into her charm offensive her biggest ally, and supporter, had been the very man she was trying not to fall for, in any way, shape or form.

In fact, she never would have been able to pull off being the Pretend Jade effectively if not for Leo. His encouragement over the last few days had been invaluable.

Trying not to let his approval mean too much had been something of an emotional minefield. Every time he looked at her with that fierce purpose in his dark gaze. Every time he touched and kissed her in public and her panties melted. Every time his lips lifted in that inscrutable smile, or something she'd done turned his deep blue eyes to a rich turquoise, she risked falling a little bit harder.

The only way to ensure Leo's attention—and

her reaction to it—didn't derail her completely had been to remember three important truths. First Leo had an agenda, second, Leo thought she was a real queen, and finally, Leo's loyalty wasn't to her—or Jade—it was to the kingdom of Severene and his role as its monarch.

Remaining aware of his emotional detachment—to his subjects as well as her—had been the best way to keep that reality front and centre. Until he'd torpedoed it approximately five minutes ago. First by finally agreeing to meet one of his subjects, then stopping dead in the barrage of camera flashes, and giving her a glimpse of a man she hadn't known existed.

He'd recovered quickly, so quickly she was fairly sure no one else had noticed. But she had... In that split second, he hadn't been Leonardo DeLessi Severo, the smart, erudite, intimidatingly cool and collected King of Severene. Or Leo the scarily gorgeous man who could turn her inside out with lust. He wasn't even Leo, the arrogant charmer who wore his confidence and his cynicism like a badge of honour...

No, for that moment suspended in time, Leo had been lost and alone and in pain.

And Juno had realised for the first time the man she thought he was wasn't the whole Leo. That was only one side of Leo. And the other side was someone who could be vulnerable too, just like her.

Her heart rammed her chest wall as the sympathy and compassion and affection for Leo she'd tried so hard not to feel overwhelmed her.

'It wasn't that cold, Leo,' she replied. 'Something upset you. Was it…? Was it something I did?' she asked, feeling guilty for the way she'd badgered him to go say hello to the little girl.

His head swung round. His lips quirked.

'Actually, yes, it was,' he said, but the devastating charm she had become so used to was gone. In its place was something studied and deliberate, almost as if he were trying to deflect the conversation. 'I'm becoming rather tired of going through the motions of this visit, without ever talking about the particulars. And I'm even more bored of sharing you with all these people.'

His gaze dipped to her mouth.

Her heart bobbled in her throat. And the hot spot between her thighs pulsed, as it always did when he looked at her mouth like that… As if he wanted to devour it in a few quick bites.

She stared right back at him. 'What happened back there? You looked…' she swallowed, the compassion making her throat hurt '…so sad.'

He blinked and then frowned. But she knew she'd hit the mark when he turned back to the view of the streets as the limousine headed back towards the palace grounds.

'Just an inconvenient moment of déjà vu,' he said, his voice rough, as if he'd had to wrench the words from his throat.

The deep frown as he continued to stare out of the car window made it obvious he wasn't seeing the huddle of traditional shops—their mullioned windows alight with Christmas lights—he was back in that moment of déjà vu.

She reached across the car and placed her hand over the fingers he had fisted on the seat between them.

He jerked round—the contact like a lightning bolt.

'If you want to talk about it, I can listen,' she said.

The furrow on his brow deepened, and for a moment she was sure she'd overstepped. But as she lifted her hand, he released the fist and captured her fingers.

'Don't…' he murmured.

His thumb stroked her knuckles, absently, as he contemplated their joined hands.

'What was it about? The moment of déjà vu?' she coaxed gently.

'Stupid really, it was so long ago. And I barely remember her.'

She squeezed his fingers, desperate to reassure, because she could hear the pain he was trying so hard to hide in the flat conversational tone of voice.

'Who?' she asked.

His gaze lifted to hers. The puzzled frown like a bear coming out of hibernation, unsure of where he was. Whatever dark place he had gone to during their walkabout, he had been back for a return trip.

'Who do you barely remember?' she asked again.

He sighed, then looked away, but he didn't let go of her hand.

'My mother,' he said on a huff of breath, so soft, she could hardly hear him.

His mother?

Juno racked her brains, trying to remember what she knew about Leo's mother. She'd met his father, as a very young child, during a state visit, and remembered she hadn't liked him. Where her father had been detached, Leo's father had been downright scary. A tall, muscular, darkly handsome man who wore his superiority like a shield and had been dismissive of her and her sister because they were girls.

But she had never met Leo's mother, because she was pretty sure the Severene Queen had died before she and her sister had even been born—which would have made Leo a very young child when his mother passed.

'She died, when you were little, didn't she?' she asked.

'Yes, a long time ago,' he said. 'Her funeral procession was held in the old town a few days after Christmas.' The frown on his forehead softened. 'Perhaps that's why today's event reminded me of it?'

'How old were you?' she asked softly, not wanting to interrupt too much. The way he was talking, she wasn't even sure he was aware of her presence.

He shrugged. 'Five, I think. The stupid thing is… I didn't know at the time, as we walked behind the casket, with the press taking photos, and the crowds staring at me, and weeping, that she was dead.'

'They made you walk behind her casket?' she said, shocked.

What kind of monster would make a child of five walk behind his own mother's coffin? No wonder Leo had an issue with connecting with his own subjects. No wonder he treated the walkabouts and other chances to meet the crowds as a chore. No wonder he had no desire to let down the mask.

'I asked my father where she was, and when he told me I started to cry. He was furious,' he said, his voice so controlled, Juno felt her heart implode.

'Why was he furious?'

He turned, his distant expression becoming quizzical. 'Hmmm?'

'Your father, what was he angry about?'

'Public displays of emotion were not permitted behaviour for a prince,' he said, his voice so distant, so controlled and unemotional, her heart broke. 'When we returned to the palace, he punished me accordingly.'

'He punished you?' The horror turned her question into a hoarse whisper. 'How?'

She'd thought he was cynical, pragmatic, even a bit of a snob, a man completely unable to connect with ordinary people, when in reality it was so much more complicated than that. Leo didn't have a superiority complex, he was wary of public displays of emotion. And now she knew why.

'By taking a riding crop to my backside.'

'He *hit* you? On the day of your mother's funeral?'

Leo's face heated at the shocked sympathy shadowing Jade's eyes. He'd said too much. Far too much. He'd never admitted his father's dedication to corporal punishment to anyone. Because it would dishonour the monarchy and embarrass him. And it was ancient history now. But it had been so hard to resist her coaxing, and the squeeze of her fingers on his.

'My father was a hard taskmaster,' he murmured. 'I think he believed it was for the best, that I needed to learn early the importance of dignity at all times.'

'But you were a five-year-old child. Who had just lost his mother, Leo. That's absolutely hideous—how could he punish you for grieving?'

He shrugged, but the movement felt stiff. Why should her compassion for that unhappy boy mean something now?

'No one ever accused him of being a kind man, or a loving father,' he said, the rawness in his throat spreading up his neck. 'But he was a well-respected king.'

As the words left his lips, they sounded hollow and inadequate.

One thing Jade had shown him in the last few days, as he'd watched her engage with the crowds, treating them as equals instead of inferiors, smiling and laughing and connecting with his subjects in a way he never had, was that his father might have been well respected, but he had never been loved. And somehow he had taken that mantel on too, not by accident, but by design. In defending himself, defending that traumatised child, he had closed himself off from all but the most tenuous contact with anyone outside his inner circle.

'Who cares if he was well respected?' she said, the certainty in her voice making his ribs ache. Her trembling fingers squeezed his hand, and his heartbeat accelerated. 'He was still a monster.'

The fierce statement had a lump forming in his throat.

A lump of raw emotion...

He swallowed heavily, trying to force it down. *Don't let her see you bleed.*

He'd become infatuated with the Queen of Monrova in the last week. Not just by her body and her scent and the way she responded to him so instinctively without even realising it. But also by her spirit, her intelligence, her smart mouth, her decidedly wicked sense of humour—and the unconventional way she seemed capable of sharing so much of herself with everyone she met.

But as she stared at him, with that fierce compassion in her eyes, and her fingers gripped his, the lump continued to grow.

'You deserved so much better,' she added. 'You were his son first and foremost, not a prince.'

He let go of her hand, and thrust his fingers

through his hair, the tight feeling in his chest becoming unbearable as the car entered the palace courtyard.

'There's no need to feel pity for that boy,' he said, struggling to talk now around the ever-expanding lump. 'He died a long time ago.'

'But, Leo, what he did is still sickening and you're still suffering because…'

'Stop…' He pressed a finger to her lips.

Her instinctive shudder of response ignited his senses in ways he understood.

'I don't wish to talk about it any more.' He couldn't talk about it. Couldn't think about that lost child. Couldn't let her see how much her defence of that child meant to him, or she would have even more power over him—and she had enough already. 'I want you, and you want me,' he said. 'Perhaps it is time to stop talking altogether?'

He clasped her face and tugged her towards him. Her hands covered his, but she didn't resist. Instead she softened against him.

He slanted his lips across hers.

This was what he needed from her, not pity or compassion, only this. And he'd waited far too long to take it.

His tongue delved deep, to capture her sob of need. The pent-up hunger of the last four days released in a rush as he gorged himself on her soft moan, her sweet mouth.

He angled her head to take the kiss deeper, to demand more. She clung to him, her fingers fisting in the cotton of his shirt, her tongue meeting his in a dance of temptation and desire.

The loud tap on the window had her jerking against his hold.

'Your Majesty, we have arrived at the palace,' the driver said through the tinted window.

'Leave the door closed,' he shouted, but he was forced to let her go.

Her hair fell around her face in disarray, her lips reddened by his kiss, her breathing as rapid as his.

'Let's stop overcomplicating this,' he said. 'I'm not a child anymore and neither are you. There's no earthly reason why we shouldn't make the most of the chemistry between us...'

Panic clouded her gaze. 'But I can't... I can't marry you, Leo, that hasn't changed.'

'To hell with the marriage,' he said.

Right now all he cared about was getting her into his bed. And stopping this need getting out of control. He'd revealed things about his past, his father, that made him feel more exposed than he had as a child, walking behind his mother's casket and feeling so alone in a crowd of strangers. That had to stop, but the only way to do that was to put this *thing* on a level he could control.

Sex was simple, uncomplicated. Emotion not so much. He had become obsessed with her; to break that obsession he needed to feed the hunger, stop trying to deny it.

'Do you...? Do you mean that?' she asked.

'You won't expect more from me if we...' he watched her throat contract as she swallowed '...if...if we become lovers?'

The wariness in her gaze made him reach out, to cup her jaw, and run his thumb across her lips.

'*If*, Jade?' he said, the surge of possessiveness undeniable when she leaned into the caress instinctively. 'Don't you mean, when?'

She pulled away from his touch, but the staggered passion in her gaze was all he needed to know.

She would be his. Before the week was out. But this was a big step for her. He needed to remember that. However instinctive her responses to him, however much she might desire him, she was innocent. He would be her first lover.

The surge of possessiveness—protectiveness even—at the thought shocked him to his core. He had never slept with a virgin before, had never wanted to, and had certainly never prized a woman's virginity. Why would he? It would be the height of hypocrisy, given that he was not a virgin himself. But somehow he couldn't deny that with Jade it was different.

He wanted to be the first man to hear her sigh, to hear her moan, to watch her come apart in his arms. But to do that, he needed to calm the hunger inside him.

'I just don't want you to think I've agreed to marry you by default,' she said. 'If we sleep together it doesn't mean more than that.'

He huffed out a strained laugh. Captivated all over again, despite his best efforts not to be. When were her honesty, her integrity, her directness going to stop surprising him?

'You have my word,' he said. '*When* we sleep together,' he corrected her again, 'it will be for our private pleasure and nothing else. The marriage is something completely separate.'

The truth was, he still planned to press the case for marriage. And he was more than willing to use their shared passion to his advantage in that regard. But he could do that at a later date. If the only way to get her into his bed now was to agree to her terms, he would do so gladly.

'*Can* we keep it private?' she asked. 'From the media? The public?'

He smiled, he couldn't help it. How could she be this naïve? After a year as a queen and even longer as a royal princess? How could she not know it would be all but impossible to keep such a liaison a secret for long? But even so he humoured her. He wasn't about to lose the chance to satisfy this maddening hunger on a technicality. 'We can certainly try.'

'When?' she asked, her directness surprising him yet again—and sending a new wave of desire south. 'When do you want to…to do it?'

Now.

He clamped down on the visceral urge to take her in the back seat of the limo.

She was putting him in charge. That she

trusted him enough to do that would have to be enough for now.

'Is that a yes, Jade?' he asked.

Her cheeks flushed a deep scarlet, but she nodded, her gaze wary but forthright. 'I... Yes, I want you too.'

He curled his fingers into fists, to stop from grabbing her as the heat pumped into his shaft.

Her forthright attitude to sex was going to kill him.

'How about after the Christmas Ball, in three days' time?' he said, thinking fast, a plan already forming that should satisfy the need for privacy. 'That's our last official engagement. It will be easier to keep our liaison private once your state visit is over.'

No one need know that she had not returned to Monrova.

Three more days of having to control his desires and limit himself to PDAs was going to be nothing short of torture—especially now she had agreed to sleep with him. But keeping this next step private was important. Once they had become lovers, he could use their physical intimacy to his advantage in any marriage negotiations, but why expose themselves before it was necessary? Surely, they both deserved a little time to enjoy this aspect of their relationship first?

'I'll make all the necessary arrangements,' he said. 'Do you trust me, Jade?'

Guilt flashed in her eyes, surprising him. What could she possibly have to feel guilty about?

'Yes,' she said. 'Yes, I do.'

He smiled, dismissing the ripple of unease. No doubt the guilt was subconscious, and a result of her father's Neanderthal attitude to marriage and virginity. After all, Andreas had boasted about his daughter's untouched state to Leo on several occasions while trying to promote a marriage between their two dynasties over the years. At the time, Leo had thought the whole concept archaic and frankly sexist, proof of a double standard that he had never adhered to.

But the irony wasn't lost on him now as his libido responded enthusiastically to Jade's guilty flush.

Not only was he turned on by the thought of being Jade's first lover, he intended to be her only lover too.

'Excellent,' he said, lifting her fingers to his lips, and buzzing a kiss across her knuckles. 'I'll see you tomorrow.'

'Won't I see you tonight?' she said, the disappointment in her voice a sop to his ego. 'For the briefing dinner?'

'Not tonight.' He tucked a knuckle under her chin, stroked the pulse point under her jaw. It fluttered deliciously. 'I think for the next three days it might be wise if we limit our meetings to public engagements. So we're not tempted to jump each other ahead of schedule.'

'Oh, yes, of course,' she said, the freckles on her nose igniting all over again. He could not wait until he got to kiss every one of those freckles. 'Then I'll see you tomorrow,' she said.

He allowed himself one last quick kiss on the tip of her nose, before turning and opening the limousine door himself.

He didn't look back as he slammed the door then headed across the courtyard towards the palace.

The next three days were going to be agony, but Jade was a precious gift who was worth the wait to unwrap.

Anticipation fired through his system—

making him feel like a child on Christmas Eve waiting for Santa to arrive, even though he'd never been allowed to believe in Santa as a child.

He would whisk Jade away to his father's old lodge. It was beautiful and secluded. And would allow them the privacy they needed—heat blasted through his system—to finally feed the hunger that had been building for the last five days. And in the days afterwards, he would have Jade all to himself to get her to accept his proposal of marriage.

CHAPTER SIX

'JUNO, IT'S SO good to hear your voice.'

Juno pressed the phone to her ear, the sound of her sister's breathless voice turning the butterflies in her stomach into a battalion.

'Sorry I couldn't get to the phone straight away,' Jade added. 'It's... It's pretty early here. And I thought we agreed we wouldn't contact each other, just in case?'

Juno had started to panic when her sister hadn't picked up immediately and the call had gone to voicemail. Why hadn't Jade answered straight away? Her sister was usually so on it, especially first thing in the morning?

Chill out, Juno. You're projecting.

'Jade... I... It's wonderful to hear you too,' she said, the sting of tears roughening her voice. She took a calming breath to beat down the butterfly battalion. 'I'm sorry I woke you up,' she added. 'And I know I'm not supposed to call, but...'

But what, exactly? Juno stalled.

She'd rehearsed this conversation a thousand times since she and Leo had agreed to a no-strings affair three days ago and she still did not know what she wanted to say to her sister...

She was so confused, so conflicted—racked with guilt and yet at the same time full of excitement, anticipation...yearning.

Agreeing to jump Leo and let him jump her tonight after the ball was wrong on so many levels it wasn't even funny but at the same time felt so right.

She had so many questions she didn't have answers to, the most glaring of which was like a ten-ton elephant that wasn't just in the room any more, it was now sitting on her chest and twirling.

Should she tell Leo who she really was before they did it? After they did it? Not at all? Wouldn't the truth risk ruining everything, not just for her, and Leo, but for Jade, too? But if she didn't tell him, would she be able to live with herself? Live with the guilt?

If this connection was just about sex, would it be so wrong to continue to pretend to be her sister? If they'd already agreed that the discussion about marriage wasn't a part of this development? And really what she'd discovered about Leo, and what Leo had discovered about her, was all true. He'd loved the way she handled herself during their engagements, and they'd found it harder and harder to keep their hands off each other in the last three days. Why couldn't tonight's ball and what happened afterwards be about who they were, instead of who they were not…?

The hypothetical arguments had spun around in her head over the last three days like out-of-control dodgems at a fairground, getting faster and faster, banging into one another, but never finding a place to stop.

'Juno, what's wrong?' her sister said, picking up on her unease from over four thousand miles away, and the hypothetical dodgems slowed, momentarily.

'Something, something's happened,' Juno blurted out. 'Something… I really did not expect…' Her voice trailed off. How to explain that combustible chemistry and the connection she'd established with Leo in the last seven days? How did she make sense of it to Jade? When she didn't really understand it herself?

'Is this about Leo, and your state visit to Severene?' her sister said. 'You make a great couple.'

'We're not a couple,' Juno said, instantly. Not only were they not a couple *yet*, but even if they became one, tonight, after the ball, as planned, it could never be more than a fleeting, physical connection. That she knew for sure.

'Are you certain?' Jade's voice was gentle, coaxing—and so devoid of judgement, the dodgems started revving their engines again. 'You look happy together in all the press coverage. And by the way you're doing a stunning job impersonating me. Better than I could do myself.'

'I'm just good at faking it,' Juno said.

'You're not faking anything, Ju, you're a natural,' her sister replied, the wistful tone confusing Juno more. 'I always told you Papa was wrong not to consider you as his successor, and now I get to say I told you so.'

'Aren't you angry with me?' Juno asked.

'Why would I be angry?' Her sister sounded genuinely puzzled.

'Because I'm not supposed to be in Severene? Because this swap was never supposed to get this complicated? Because I could end up completely screwing up Monrova's diplomatic relationship with Severene.'

If Leo found out who she really was—and went ballistic—which was a distinct possibility.

The truth was, she had no real clue how Leo would react.

He might think it was funny, sexy, cool. But what if he didn't? What if he got super mad and ended up hating her? What if it caused a diplomatic incident? And he punished Jade, too? If this was just about sex would it be better never to tell him the truth? Just in case? To protect herself and her sister? She'd been rejected before, she knew just how much that hurt. And did she really have the right to risk Jade's reputation, when she had been the one to push for this swap in the first place?

Every day she'd kept the secret, every day she'd got closer to Leo, discovered more about him, and herself, the stakes had got higher. It had never been her intention to hurt anyone. But in the last week, all the possible ramifications of what could happen if she told Leo the truth—good and bad—had begun to torture her.

Three days ago, Leo's offer of a private no-strings fling had seemed like the perfect solution. If the marriage was off the table, how could sleeping with him do any harm?

And Leo was the one who had suggested it.

Now every time he looked at her as if he wanted to devour her, and she melted in response; every time he winked at her or smiled at her, and she became breathless; every time she looked at him and saw the traumatised child as well as the man he had become, she knew this thing between them was about her and Leo, not Jade and Leo, and certainly not some arranged marriage...

'No, I'm not angry about any of that,' her sister said at last, interrupting Juno's frantic qualifications. 'I've come to realise, seeing the press reports of you two, that Leo and I were never meant to be together,' Jade added. 'I'm really glad you persuaded me to come to New York.' She paused. 'It's been an eye-opening experience for me. I also think it's super cute that there seems to be something developing between you two.'

'There's nothing developing between us. Nothing permanent anyway,' Juno murmured.

Whether she told Leo who she really was or

not, nothing could come of their liaison. 'It's just... There's a lot of chemistry between us,' she said. 'And I like him more than I ever expected to.'

Leo wasn't the man she had thought he was. He had depth and layers, he was complicated, with a past not nearly as easy and entitled as she had assumed. He had struggled with his place in the world, just as she had. In fact, he'd struggled more.

She had been dismissed by her father because she was never going to be Queen, and King Andreas had considered his responsibilities to the Crown more important than his responsibilities to his daughters. But Leo had been abused by his own father; if King Constantin had believed that maintaining a dignified front at a funeral mattered more than comforting a grieving child she very much doubted it was the only time he had hit his son.

Their shared pain had given them a connection—but they had dealt with that pain in very different ways. While she had rejected her royal heritage and reacted to her father's neglect by being more rebellious, more reckless, more irresponsible, Leo had done the opposite. He didn't even seem to acknowledge the extent of his father's abuse, nor did he resent his duty to the Crown. And while a week ago she would have thought less of him for that, now she felt more. She'd watched Leo in the last week taking on his responsibilities, refusing to shirk them, even though she now knew how hard some of that was for him. And that had made her think of Jade too, and how Jade had done the same.

While Juno had always taken the easy route, the selfish route, the path of least resistance and done precisely what she chose.

If this week with Leo had done one thing, it had given her a maturity she hadn't realised she lacked. Made her realise there was more to life than personal freedom, that some things were bigger than yourself. Leo had taught her that. And she hoped in return she'd helped Leo to lighten up a little, to not take every element of his job so seriously, and to forgive that little boy for crying at his mother's funeral.

'Are you sure there's nothing more between you?' Jade said, sounding wistful. 'From the press reports I've seen, he looks at you in a way he's never looked at any of the other women he's dated.'

Juno's heart galloped into her throat at the softly spoken question. She swallowed heavily, trying to push down the foolish bubble of hope.

That's because he thinks I'm a real queen.

'No, there's nothing more,' she said.

Don't go getting even more delusional than you are already, Ju.

As much as she had come to care for Leo, anything more than satisfying the chemistry that had been driving them both nuts for seven days was not going to happen. Because she would always be a fake… And he was the real deal.

'Jade, I just…' Juno began again. *Just get to the point.* 'What I need to know, the reason I called, is…' Juno swallowed—could this actually get any more awkward? 'If Leo and I jump each other tonight. I mean, he's asked me and I… I really want to go for it. Because, you know, chemistry,' she said, trying to sound pragmatic when she was struggling to breathe. 'We've agreed it won't mean anything beyond the physical. That it won't have any political implications. That the marriage is a whole separate issue. But if you'd rather we didn't… I mean, I don't want to mess things up for you… With Leo.'

'Juno, you're not serious—what possible claim would I have on Leonardo?'

'Well, you know, you were considering marrying him a week ago,' Juno said.

Jade laughed, interrupting Juno's guilt trip.

'The marriage was always just about securing a trade relationship and uniting our two kingdoms,' Jade said easily enough. 'I can't believe I ever thought that would be okay.'

'Jade, you don't sound like yourself,' Juno said, noticing the strange tone in her sister's voice for the first time, a tone she'd never heard before. Jade had always been so certain about her role in life, her duties and responsibilities. Juno had wanted to shake things up with this swap, but now she wondered if she'd shaken them up too much. 'Are you sure everything is going okay in New York?'

As usual she'd made this call about her. Why hadn't she asked Jade for details about what was happening Stateside?

'It's… Yes, it's been really transformative in a lot of ways,' Jade said, but Juno couldn't tell from her sister's tone whether that was a good thing, or not.

Juno's concern increased.

'I'm discovering things about myself I didn't realise,' Jade added. 'Not all of which I like.'

'What things?' Juno asked, getting more concerned by the second. 'There's nothing about you not to like.'

'I used to think the same thing.' Jade laughed again, but the brittle note jarred.

'If something's happened, Jade, you can tell me, or we could swap back. Now.'

'No. I don't want to swap back, not yet. I'd really like to stay until New Year's Eve, like we agreed,' Jade added. 'Unless you want to...'

'No, I don't want to swap back yet either,' Juno admitted, glad that Jade at least seemed very sure about staying in New York as long as they'd originally agreed.

'Listen, Ju, I've got to go,' her sister said. 'I've got a busy day ahead of me. But whatever you and Leo do, or don't do, you have my blessing. Okay?'

'Okay,' she said, knowing she should be pleased her sister had given her carte blanche to do whatever she wanted with Leo tonight.

'But do me a favour, don't underestimate your feelings for him,' Jade added. 'They might be stronger than you think.'

Before Juno could reply, the line was dead, and her sister was gone.

Juno's heart rate increased as she put down the phone. The giddy rush of anticipation at what tonight might bring ramping up.

But as she spent the next hours getting primped and prepped to within an inch of her life, she couldn't shake the growing feeling of vertigo, as if she were standing on the edge of a precipice and Jade's blessing had just brought her one step closer to the fall.

CHAPTER SEVEN

THE CHRISTMAS BALL was Severene's pre-
miere event of the year and one of Europe's
most sought-after social occasions. Dignitaries
and VIPs, politicians and A-list celebrities were
flown in from all over the globe to attend. The
palace ballroom—considerably larger than the
one in Monrova—glowed with the twinkle of a
thousand tiny lights, the walls festooned with
ribbon and garlands, silver baubles and gold
leaves, to ring in the festive season. A thirty-
foot fir tree from Severene's pine forest stood
like a beacon in the far corner aglow with green
fairy lights and scarlet bows.

Beautiful people danced to a thirty-piece orchestra in the main ballroom, and mingled in
the adjacent antechambers while being served
cordon-bleu cuisine created by a battalion of
Michelin-starred chefs and vintage champagne
and wine curated by a world-renowned som-
melier.

Juno floated through the evening on a wave of desperate hope and frantic excitement—while burying the unanswered questions deep.

As soon as Leo's hand had folded over hers at the top of the wide sweeping staircase, where they were the last guests to be announced, and he led her down onto the marble floor of the ballroom, she'd made a conscious decision to live for the moment and deal with the decisions she had to make on an as and when basis.

She would play it by ear. Figure out what was the right thing to do when she needed to, and not before. Tonight was about living the dream and forgetting about the reality. Whatever happened it would be her last night with Leo; tomorrow she had to return to Monrova and, whether she told him who she really was or not, she could never see him again.

Whatever she did or didn't tell Leo though, it gave her a giddy thrill to know that no one here even suspected a girl from Queens was masquerading as a queen among them tonight.

See, Father, for all my wild ways, I could have made a good queen. Just not your sort of queen.

Leo monopolised every one of her dances,

and she could see the assembled throng going glassy-eyed at the romantic couple they made. Him in his red dress uniform, and her in a ball gown of rich emerald velvet that matched her eyes.

Their romance might be fake, but tonight the fairy tale felt real. And even if none of these people would ever know who she really was, she would know. And that was enough.

He'd helped her to prove her father wrong. And that mattered, even if tonight was their last night together.

She would miss him. In many ways he was the ultimate Prince Charming, handsome, dashing, demanding, unknowable, larger than life in every respect. But she couldn't fall into the same trap as her mother—believing she could have more—when this was all there was.

She'd seen the press photos from the Christmas Ball over the years, a ball her sister had rarely attended, and locked the yearning to be here inside her—determined to believe she didn't want the life that had been denied her. But tonight she could indulge every single one of those secret desires.

As the guest of honour at the ball, she had

to mix and mingle, but Leo made no secret of the fact he wanted her in his arms as often as possible, so their royal duties were cut to a minimum.

Giddy with her new confidence, Juno fed on the adrenaline rush as he whisked her round under the twinkle of lights, and they played out the last of her Cinderella fantasy.

Anticipation skittered over her skin, every time his strong arms held her a little too close, or his subtle cologne filled her lungs, or his large hand rested on the small of her back.

As the clock struck midnight, and the revellers let up a cheer, a golden sleigh was hauled into the centre of the ballroom by six footmen, loaded down with elaborately wrapped gifts. As the guests began to help themselves, sighing and gasping at the kingdom's largesse, Leo grasped Juno's hand and tugged her towards the staircase they had descended together four hours before.

The adrenaline rush became turbocharged. Finally, they could be alone. The ball would wind down now, her state visit over. And the night they had committed to three days ago could begin.

There was nothing to stop them doing whatever they wanted into the early hours of the morning—and no one to see it.

He leaned down, his hand settling on her back, and whispered against her ear: 'I have to say goodnight to a load of boring diplomats. But I'll see you upstairs in fifteen minutes.'

The intense gaze that had been focussed on her all evening made her pulse jump and jitter. 'But I'll need to get Jennie to help me get out of this gown,' she said.

His gaze dropped to her cleavage, and the emerald velvet compressed her ribs. 'Give her the night off. Getting you out of that gown is a job I've been looking forward to all evening.'

Bowing, he made a point of kissing her knuckles and bidding her a formal goodnight. The camera clicks from a nearby photographer faded into the background, as Juno's heart pummelled her chest in hard, heavy thuds.

She watched him disappear into the crowd. She would have to tell him who she really was. But did she have to tell him right away?

She waited the required five minutes to cover the fact they were leaving together, then summoned Serena. Ten frustrating minutes later, she had said all the necessary goodbyes and headed up the stairs towards her suite of rooms, so hyped she could hardly breathe.

There had been no sign of Leo. She hoped he had managed to escape faster than she had. And that he was waiting for her as planned. She didn't want to have too much time to think alone in her rooms.

As she took the last turning towards her suite, a warm hand clasped her wrist and tugged her to a stop.

'About damn time, what took you so long?'

Leo! Her heart bounced into her throat.

She struggled to keep pace with his long strides as he led her down the hallway, past the double doors leading to her private suite.

'Where are we going?' she managed as she stumbled.

He paused just long enough to scoop her off her feet.

'To my rooms,' he said, his voice so husky, the wry, mocking tone had become raw.

She knew how he felt as she clung to his shoulders.

'Where I intend to ravish you,' he added,

marching towards his suite with purpose in every stride.

The hot sweet spot between her thighs burned as her breath released.

Ravish! Did he just say ravish?

The last coherent thought flew out of her head and she leapt over the edge of the precipice.

Did it really matter who she was?

Surely all that mattered right now was feeding this hunger?

'The Severene monarchy…i.e. me…has some standards,' Leo growled as he carried Jade down the corridor to his suite of rooms. 'And *not* popping the Queen of Monrova's cherry in a corridor happens to be one of them.'

Did you actually just refer to popping the Queen's cherry?

But as Jade smothered a shocked laugh against his chest—and he finally reached the sanctuary of his rooms—Leo decided he'd be damned if he would apologise for the crude language.

The woman had bewitched him, and the only way to break the enchantment was to give them both what they'd waited far too long for already.

The velvet gown glided under his hands as he placed her on her feet, but the feel of her firm, toned body beneath, the lush curves shivering under his touch, sent the twist of need into his gut.

How had she managed to stay a virgin for twenty-four years?

Doesn't matter.

She was his now, and only his. And he was glad she'd waited. Because he wanted to be the first man to uncover her secrets.

He started with the diamond tiara, which he had dreamed of divesting her of a week ago on the balcony in Monrova. Locating the pins in the room's half-light, he plucked them out of her elaborate hairdo to toss them across the room.

She sighed as he lifted the jewelled head-piece and dumped it on a nearby chair. He took off his jacket, unbuttoned his shirt as her hair tumbled down in a glorious wave of chestnut curls. Her breathing became fast and jagged as he lost his shirt.

Clasping her neck, he caught the silky locks at her nape, and dragged her mouth to his. Her lips softened, her moan making his erection throb as the kiss became deep and elemental. His tongue tangled with hers, exploiting, demanding, so hungry for the taste of her he doubted he would ever be sated.

He ripped his lips away first and drew a staggered breath. Her eyes fixed on his, glazed with lust and longing, but also shadowed with what he could only assume was shock.

Slow down, be gentle.

He'd joked about ravishing her, but it didn't seem funny any more. The fact of her virginity roared in his head, as he gathered every last ounce of his control to force the words out of his mouth.

'Are you sure this is what you want?' he murmured. 'I don't want to hurt you.'

For a moment he saw guilt flash across her face—which made no sense—but then she said, 'You won't.'

His hands were clumsy in his urgency to locate the zip on her gown. The sibilant hum as he drew it down seemed deafening above the crackle of the fire and her staggered breathing.

The velvet slid down to collect in an emerald pool at her feet, revealing a banquet of treasures even more breathtaking than he had imagined.

Damn, but she was exquisite. The swatches of purple lace did nothing to disguise the shadow of her areolae and the neat triangle of hair at the apex of her thighs.

How could he have been so unmoved by her beauty a month ago? When he had become obsessed in the last week with gorging himself on every gorgeous inch?

The last molecules of blood still in his brain pounded beneath his belt, the desire to claim her so powerful and all-consuming his body burned. He unhooked the front fastening of her bra and stifled a moan as her breasts spilled into his palms.

He cradled the swollen flesh, circling the rigid peaks with his thumbs. His erection stiffened to iron as her sobs became pants of need. He bent to capture one plump nipple in his mouth, drowning in her delicious scent, determined to prolong the torture for them both as long as was humanly possible.

Her fingers fisted in his hair, tugging and pulling as she begged. 'Please… I need more.'

The last threads on his control snapped at her breathless plea. Leaving the banquet of fragrant flesh, he lifted her into his arms and carried her through the suite's living room and into his bedroom.

He placed her on the large four-poster bed in the centre of the room. He watched her watching him, her chestnut curls rioting around her head, her beautiful body pale against the golden quilt, the ripe flesh gilded by the firelight as he stripped off the last of his clothing.

Her dark emerald gaze drifted down, and the flush on her cheeks darkened.

He was a large man in every respect and her wary look gave him a moment of concern.

'Don't worry,' he said. 'I promise to be gentle.'

Her gaze met his. 'You don't need to be gentle,' she said, the fearless comment as bold and brave as the rest of her.

His heart swelled, making his ribs feel uncomfortably tight. He shook off the unfamiliar emotion and climbed on the bed. After dragging off her panties, he cupped her to capture the wet heat.

This was sex, and phenomenal chemistry. He liked her, had grown accustomed to having her by his side, and she had made the usual roster of Christmas engagements less of a chore than usual in the last week. But he didn't require more, and certainly didn't want more.

She bucked as he delved, circling, testing, his thumb finding the slick nub of her clitoris. She writhed as he exploited it, drawing forth her sobs. Watching her enjoy her own pleasure was so erotic he had to grit his teeth to stop from embarrassing himself.

'Come for me,' he demanded, and she responded instinctively, her body bowing back as she shattered.

His heart thundered in his chest, his ribs like a vice now as he positioned her hips. Her eyes fluttered open, dazed with afterglow as he notched the head of his erection at her entrance and pushed.

She was unbearably hot, unbearably tight, her sex clamped around him, but her body stretched to receive him, her nails scoring his shoulders, her pants becoming sobs as he pressed deep.

'Are you okay?' he managed.

She hadn't flinched. And he hadn't felt any impediment.

Puzzling questions clouded his mind, but then she nodded, and the need for answers dimmed.

He had to move, to claim her fully, before he exploded.

Clasping her hips, he rocked out, then thrust back, filling her to the hilt this time. He continued to move, slow and careful at first, still mindful of his size, digging deep to work her G-spot. He established a brutal rhythm, clenched his teeth to ignore the orgasm licking at the base of his spine. Desperate to hold on, determined to make her shatter first. And brand her as his.

His Queen, *his* woman, *his* lover.

She cried out, the vicious pulse of her climax triggering his own unstoppable release.

His seed exploded into her womb as he soared over the high wide ledge and let himself fall.

Sweaty, exhausted, sated, he collapsed into her welcoming embrace, drenched in a pleasure so intense, so fierce, he was afraid he might never be able to get enough of it.

Juno's eyes drifted open. Dazed, disorientated and floating in a shiny sea of afterglow, she lay cocooned in a delicious cloud of sandalwood cologne and man.

Her tender sex twitched and she became brutally aware of the thick intrusion, still firm, still *there* inside the tight clasp of her body.

The heavy weight pressing into her collarbone grunted.

'Stop that, or I'll have to ravish you again, and it will probably kill us both.'

Her instinctive chuckle at the wry observation choked off as the delirious fog dissolved. And a strange new reality came flooding in.

The man lying on top of her, his black hair illuminated by the firelight, his masculine scent intoxicating, had just given her so much more than she had thought possible.

A vicious shudder racked her body and she had to bite down on her lip, hard enough to taste blood, to stop the shocked sob buried in her chest rising up her throat.

Emotion slammed into her like a freight train.

What had she done? She had known sex with Leo would be good, the best she'd ever had. Because that wasn't much of a competition.

But she hadn't expected it to mean anything more than that. And yet it had. Because as well as the stupendous, breathtaking orgasms, there had been the staggering wave of intimacy.

'Hey, what's wrong, Jade?' he murmured, the

gruff use of her sister's name only making her feel more exposed. More compromised.

She hadn't told him the truth. Had convinced herself it didn't matter. And now suddenly it did.

Her flesh released him with difficulty as he withdrew.

He frowned and cradled her cheek. 'Did I hurt you?'

She shook her head, unable to speak past the huge boulder forming in her throat.

She'd ruined everything. She had never thought sex could be so overwhelming.

And now she had to deal with the consequences.

She'd always been impulsive. And she'd paid a high price for that in the past. But this time, *this* time, she'd gone too far, way too far to ever be forgiven.

'Speak to me, Jade,' he said, brushing his thumb down the side of her face, shaming her even more as brutal yearning echoed in her sex. 'You need to tell me what's wrong.'

'I... I...' The tenderness and concern in his expression only shamed her more. She'd lied to him, convinced herself it was just a little lie, a convenient omission, but now she knew it wasn't. 'Really, I'm fine,' she managed. She pulled his hand away from her face, so she could move away from him.

The flight instinct was a familiar one. So she went with it.

She needed to think, figure out how to break the news to him—that she wasn't the woman he thought she was.

She scooted off the bed, brutally aware of the sticky residue of their lovemaking. He hadn't used a condom.

Doesn't matter. You can deal with that later, once you've told him the truth.

Her heart lodged in her throat. But how did she do that? He had treated her with such respect, such warmth, such care, and it was all based on a lie. She'd seen the puzzled look cross his face when he'd entered her, had known in that instant exactly what he was thinking.

Why isn't she a virgin?

She made it to the edge of the bed, swung her legs to the floor, but just as she prepared to make a dash for the bathroom he grasped her wrist.

'Everything's not okay, Jade,' he stated, his

voice strained but firm, his frown deepening. 'That much is obvious.'

Please stop calling me that. I'm not Jade, I'm Juno.

'If I hurt you, if I was too rough with you, you need to tell me,' he said.

Please, just stop.

'You didn't… You didn't hurt me, Leo. The sex was phenomenal… It's just, I've never had an orgasm during sex before and…' A blush blazed into her cheeks as she babbled to a halt. Had she just admitted that? Out loud?

'Before?' he said. He didn't sound angry or upset, simply surprised. Even so, she wanted to curl up into a ball and die. 'So I wasn't your first?'

'Yes, I mean, no. There was only one other guy. When I was sixteen in high school,' she said. At least this was the truth.

'But no orgasms?' he asked and she noticed the slight quirk of his lips. Was that good? Even if she felt brutally humiliated?

'He'd bet his pals he could deflower a princess,' she said, forcing herself to give him the miserable details of that furtive, uncomfortable night eight years ago, which had left her feeling sore and dissatisfied. Brad had boasted to his friends that the Princess wasn't all that. And she'd been forced to take the walk of shame the next day in gym class. She'd held her head up and ignored the sniggers, and the scathing looks. She'd done nothing wrong—why should she be ashamed? Brad had been the villain in that scenario. The liar.

But she was the liar now.

'It made me think sex was totally overrated. And I thought it always had to be like that...'

The sensual smile on Leo's lips became more than a little smug.

Shut up. This isn't helping.

He squeezed her wrist and rubbed his thumb across her rampaging pulse.

'The guy sounds like a bastard, Jade,' he murmured. 'I'm glad I got to be your first in the only way that matters.'

The comment was kind, when she knew she didn't deserve kind.

'It was a long time ago, now,' she said, staring down at her hands, aware of her nakedness. 'I can barely remember him.'

Tucking a knuckle under her chin, Leo lifted her face. 'I'm glad I didn't hurt you,' he said gently. 'Although if you'd told me sooner we could have jumped each other three days ago.'

Her heart scrambled. Really? That was why he'd suggested waiting? Because he'd been concerned about her virginity? The wave of tenderness built again.

Followed by the nauseous wave of guilt. She had to tell him the truth. She'd lied and lied, to him and to herself, because she'd wanted this to happen. But now it had, every single one of those qualifications and justifications and excuses had been exposed for what they were— bare-faced, self-serving lies, so she could trick a king into seducing her.

'I... You thought I was a virgin,' she said, trying not to wince. 'I'm sorry.'

'Your father boasted about your untouched state quite a lot.' The mild amusement in his tone only damned her more. 'I guess he didn't know about the bastard.' His brow furrowed, his gaze direct and probing. 'When did you go to high school? I always thought you were homeschooled, like me?' The quizzical tone, and the easy affection behind it, made panic tighten around her ribs.

Tell him. Tell him now.

But somehow the words wouldn't come out of her mouth. Instead her heart rammed her throat and started to choke her. Her mind whirred in frantic circles, accelerating like a merry-go-round spinning out of control.

His grip tightened and he moved to sit next to her. His naked hip bumped hers as he placed his hand on her back. And rubbed.

'Breathe, Jade,' he murmured.

She sucked in a juddering breath past constricted lungs, his voice an anchor as the merry-go-round juddered and jumped and finally started to slow.

'I'm sorry,' she mumbled, dropping her head into her hands. 'This is super awkward.'

'Awkward?' He gave a husky chuckle. 'I disagree.' He tucked a lock of hair behind her ear. She turned her head at the gentle touch, to find him watching her. 'More like fascinating and charming,' he murmured, the rough appreciation in his tone making her heart swell painfully in her chest again. 'You just keep surprising me, Jade.'

You have no idea.

Her sister's name knifed into her gut and she

straightened. 'I'm so, so sorry, Leo,' she said, because what else could she say?

Her mind began to race through all the possible ways to tell him what she should have told him ten minutes ago. Ten hours ago. A week ago. As soon as she'd kissed him on the snow-covered balcony, let him bare her breast in the frozen night and set them on this path.

I'm not Jade, I'm Juno. I went to high school in New York. Because I'm a nobody, not a queen. Jade's the virgin, not me.

'Don't be sorry.' The sensual smile made her heart leap in her chest. 'I'm not,' he continued, his thumb resting on the rioting pulse in her collarbone. 'In fact, I'm probably the one who should apologise.' His blue eyes focussed on her face, the sincerity making her stomach tangle into a knot. 'I didn't use a condom. And I didn't ask if you're using birth control?'

'Umm... No, but we should be okay, my period is due very soon,' she whispered.

Could this actually get any more awkward?

'Maybe we don't have to worry either way.' He smiled. 'After how good that just was, my offer of a union between us is still very much on the table.' Bracketing her hips, he drew her towards him.

What?

Just as her panic started to spiral out of control again, he pressed his lips to the rioting pulse in her collarbone. She jolted, let out a broken sigh, the tantalising butterfly kisses making the heavy weight in her stomach sink into her sex.

He lifted his head, cradled her cheeks.

'How about you stay here and we can negotiate the details over the holiday?' he said, his mouth hovering over hers. 'I thought we could take a trip to my father's old hunting lodge. It's secluded, and private, and it will give us a chance to get to know each other even better.' He lifted his brows, the heat in his gaze making her want to cry.

That sounded so good, but it could never happen.

She flattened her palms against his chest as he lowered his head. The misery helping to smother the knot of shame as heat bloomed in her core.

'Stop, Leo. We can't.' She pushed him away.

'No?' he said, the confident, mocking tone

making the knot in her gut grow to impossible proportions.

'I told you, we can't get married,' she blurted out. 'Ever. I told you that before I agreed to tonight.'

'Why not?' His lips twisted and the devastating smile did crazy things to her equilibrium. 'We're terrific together, in every way that counts. We just proved that beyond a doubt.'

You have to tell him. Now.

But how?

She'd screwed up so badly, she didn't know if there was a way to make this right.

'I need to take a shower.' *A cold shower. A very long, very cold shower.*

'Do you want me to join you?' he said, in that too sexy voice that made her want to say yes, when she knew she couldn't.

'Maybe next time,' she said, as she shot off the bed and made a dash for the bathroom.

She slammed the door and pressed her back against it. His confused look at her erratic behaviour imprinted on her brain.

She was a coward, as well as a liar, but she had to figure out the right way to tell him the whole truth and nothing but the truth—to minimise the enormity of her betrayal. And she couldn't do that while he was looking at her as if he wanted to devour her, and her sex was still humming from the feel of him deep inside her.

She jumped as the door bumped against her back. 'Jade, what's going on? Can I come in?'

'Nothing, *really*, I just need a minute...' *Or fifty.* 'I'll be out soon.'

As soon as I've figured out how to defend the indefensible.

CHAPTER EIGHT

LEO RESTED HIS forehead against the bathroom door. He heard the shower and realised he had been dismissed. He frowned.

The woman was more capricious than a wild stallion, but while Jade's unpredictable moods had been a major turn-on for days now—hell, ever since he'd seen her marching towards him at the Winter Ball a week ago with that bold, reckless light shining in her eyes—the trickle of unease had started to become a flood.

Something about this whole thing didn't add up. Had never added up. He'd dismissed that gut instinct a week ago, and every day since, because he'd wanted her, more than he'd ever wanted any woman. She had captivated him, bewitched him even, and the sex they'd just shared had been... Frankly, mind-blowing.

But that realisation only made his uneasiness increase.

He'd never had a sexual experience like it...

One so intense he hadn't even remembered to use protection. He'd had a couple of condoms burning a hole in the pocket of his jacket all evening, but when he'd watched her body brace with pleasure, the need to bury himself deep inside her had been so overwhelming he hadn't stopped to think.

She'd been artless and eager, responsive to every touch, every taste, every look, the chemistry between them as explosive as ever. And she hadn't been experienced, but at the same time he wasn't her first.

He had wanted to throttle the bastard who she had lost her virginity to—and wished that it could have been him—which didn't make a lot of sense either.

The questions just kept coming—the inconsistencies, the surprises, the strange feeling of déjà vu that first time he'd kissed her.

Why had she seemed so naïve and insecure about her role as Queen? Why had she been so unconventional in her approach to their royal duties, when she had seemed to be so serene and controlled when he had met her on previous occasions? Why had she turned him inside out with lust, and longing, this week, when she never had before? Why had he trusted her so easily with the truth about his father, blurted out all that revealing stuff about his mother's funeral? And why had the mention of marriage caused her to freak out, when she'd discussed the offer with such pragmatism less than a month ago?

So many questions. Questions he'd put to one side but which were bombarding him now. Questions he needed answers to.

He walked back to the bed, scooped up his boxers and trousers and put them on. The sound of pounding water from the power shower covered the click as he tried the bathroom door.

It wasn't locked. He stepped into the room.

She stood in the shower cubicle, with her back to him.

Soap suds slid over skin flushed pink under the pummelling jets and the familiar heat pounded back to life. He sank his fists into his pockets and leant back against the door to enjoy the show. He needed to calm down before he quizzed her.

He'd always been a cynical man, but whatever was going on here, it probably had a reasonable explanation.

She went about the ritual of washing all those beautiful curves. And he had the strange thought he could happily spend the rest of his life watching a show like this every morning.

Strange, because, even though tonight had only confirmed for him how much potential a marriage between them had, he doubted even the stupendous chemistry they shared would lead to a lifelong commitment to his royal wife.

He just wasn't built for that kind of emotional investment...

He had wanted this marriage, not just because of the diplomatic and financial benefits for both their monarchies, but also because a marriage based on expediencies would not require him to give more than he was capable of. This week's events, though, had created something of a problem in that regard, because Jade intrigued and fascinated him enough to complicate his feelings towards her.

Not only did he want her more than expected, he was now even more invested in getting her to agree to the marriage.

She lifted her arms to finish rinsing the shampoo from her hair, giving him a tantalising view of her breast in profile, the puckered nipple still reddened by his attentions.

The heat spiked and he forced himself to banish the unhelpful thoughts. Just because he wanted her, in bed as well as out, theirs would still have to be a marriage of convenience.

'We can't get married. Ever.'

He recalled the panicked expression on her face when she'd refused him. Again.

Why couldn't she marry him? She hadn't given him an answer.

The flood of unease helped to dampen the heat as she switched off the jets and reached for the pile of towels on the vanity. The steam that had obscured his vision was sucked away, giving him a view of every luscious inch as she dried herself.

She bent forward to dry her legs, and he spotted something on her hip that he hadn't noticed in the shadows of the bedroom.

What was that? A birthmark? No, a tattoo... A faded tattoo of a unicorn...

His heartbeat kicked up another notch, and the erection stiffened.

Jade had a tattoo... Of a unicorn? How had she managed to get that past her father?

'I love unicorns, they're a symbol of magic and freedom. I think I'm going to get a tattoo of one as soon as it's legal.'

The passionate voice of another princess stabbed at his consciousness from eight long years ago.

What the...?

The shocking truth barrelled into him—and the knot in his gut became a nuclear bomb.

He shuddered so violently, the door behind him rattled against the frame.

She swung round, letting out a shocked gasp as she clasped the towel to her chest.

'Leo? How long have you been standing there?'

Rage rose up his torso as he strode across the bathroom, positively shaking now. He'd been taken for a fool. Tricked, exploited and humiliated.

'Long enough,' he ground out, the rage all but choking him as he grasped her wrist and tugged her towards him, so he could re-examine the evidence up close.

He swore, furious that the sight of her bottom—and the saucy mythical creature etched into her skin in faded colours—caused the inevitable rush of desire.

'Leo, stop.' She wrestled her arm free and scrambled to cover her backside from his inspection. But she couldn't disguise the guilty flush burning across her collarbone and spreading up her neck. Or the panic darkening those emerald eyes. Panic he'd been so desperate to soothe five minutes ago, after they'd made love. Panic that suddenly made sense now too.

He fisted his fingers, stuffed them into his pockets, to resist the urge to throw her over his knee and give her the spanking she deserved.

Breathe, damn it.

'Why?' The one word came out on a broken breath, only humiliating him more. He fought off the twist of pain in his gut, forced the fury to the fore, to cover it. He'd told her things he should never have told anyone. She'd tricked him, manipulated him, lied to him, but he'd let her. '*Why* did you do it? Why did you lie to me for seven days straight? Is this some kind of sick joke?'

Kiss me, Leo. You know you want to.

The memory came flooding back, and with it the hurt that had shadowed her eyes when he'd told her he didn't want her. And suddenly he knew. His fury became huge and all-consuming, but it still couldn't cover the ache in his belly.

'It was payback, wasn't it? Because I refused to kiss you all those years ago. Well, congratulations, Princess Juno, you got me.'

The horrified guilt in her eyes gave him a grim sense of satisfaction, but did nothing to ease the pain in his gut.

It had all been a lie. Every damn thing. He'd been captivated, enchanted, overwhelmed... And she'd been laughing at him all along.

'I... I'm sorry,' Juno sputtered, but the apology felt weak at best. And no defence against his fury.

Her mind raced to catch up with her accelerating pulse and the anxiety threatening to close off her air supply.

His eyes narrowed. 'You're *sorry*?' The scathing look burned into her skin. 'You were always a spoilt, wilful brat, but this... This is something else.'

The insult cut through all her tough-girl bravado to the child she'd been, branded the Problem Princess and kicked out of the palace by her father.

'I know I should have said something sooner.' She wrapped the towel around herself, but how could she shield herself from his judgement, and how could she protect her heart from the great big black hole forming in her chest and threatening to suck away the last of her confidence and self-respect?

She deserved this. She knew that. She'd been a liar and a coward, he was right. But hadn't any of it been real? Not one thing? Where was the man who had looked at her with such approval, such hunger, such tenderness?

'I wanted to tell you, but I was scared you wouldn't... That you wouldn't...'

'That I wouldn't what?' He sank his fists deeper into his pants pockets, making his pecs bulge and tense.

She could feel his fury pumping off him in waves. Unfortunately it wasn't the only heat she could feel.

Fire flared through her oversensitised body, tightening her nipples into hard peaks and sinking like a heavy weight deep into her abdomen.

She edged back a step, her butt bumping into

the vanity, disgusted and humiliated by her body's response.

'What?' he barked, making her jump.

'That you wouldn't want me...' she said, the broken sob of need impossible to disguise. 'The way I wanted you.'

They were both breathing too fast, the vicious arousal darkening his gaze as real and vivid as the melting sensation going molten at her core. But she knew, even though she'd only just acknowledged it, this had never been just a physical need.

Why hadn't she had the courage to admit that to herself until now?

'It was never you I wanted though, was it?' he ground out, stepping away as if she were contaminated. 'It was your sister.'

The rejection lanced into her heart, cutting through every last one of her defences. Defences she had built up over years, to seal herself away from the pain.

She looked down. So ashamed now she felt as if her heart were being ripped out of her chest. 'I know,' she said.

Who the heck had she been kidding? How could what she felt for him, what she had hoped he felt for her, ever have been authentic when it had always been based on a lie?

'Do you have any idea what you've done?' he snarled.

'I'm so sorry,' she said again, her voice a whisper of pain.

He grasped her chin, dragged her gaze up to his. 'Sorry isn't good enough,' he growled, the controlled fury in his tone making her flinch.

Her breath got trapped in her throat as the panic and pain roiled in her gut.

'I know,' she said. 'But I'm still sorry that you hate me now.'

I don't hate you. I wish I did.

The truth bounced into Leo's brain, but he managed to stop himself from voicing it. Juno Monroyale had caused this crisis, with her asinine little charade, and he'd be damned if he'd let her get away with her thoughtless, reckless behaviour.

Maybe he didn't hate her. How could he, when she had been so vibrant, so alive and intoxicating in his bed? When he still wanted her so much? And when a part of him couldn't seem to get it through his head that the woman who had captivated him had never been real... in any of her guises?

Not the fierce goddess who had protected a freezing footman. Not the natural nurturer who had crouched down to charm a little girl. Not the compassionate friend who had comforted the lonely boy who still lurked inside him.

But even if there was some truth in there somewhere, how could those women make up for the one who lurked beneath all of those guises? The spoilt brat who had never had to give a damn about anyone but herself.

While the real Jade had stayed in Monrova and been groomed to become Queen, her twin sister—from what he could remember of what he'd read about her over the years—had swanned off to New York with her feckless mother and become the darling of Manhattan high society, carving out a niche for herself as the Rebel Princess on social media that was as vacuous and self-absorbed as she was.

Perhaps it was about time the Rebel Princess learned actions had consequences. That honour and duty meant something. And that being of royal blood gave you responsibilities, not a licence to do precisely what you chose.

Nobody knew that more than he did; he'd had that mantra literally beaten into him by his own father. And he'd be damned if he'd allow Juno's latest prank to have any lasting impact on him or his monarchy—which meant keeping this disaster out of the public domain, by whatever means necessary.

'Where is your sister?' he demanded, disgusted all over again that he'd been forced into this position. How was he supposed to clean up the mess she'd made?

'In New York, pretending to be me.'

'So she was in on this too?' he said, not sure whether Jade's involvement made him even madder or not. 'Whose idea was it?'

'Mine,' she said.

'Figures.' He stared. Why was he not surprised?

'We swapped places on the afternoon of the Winter Ball. It wasn't really planned, it just sort of happened. The idea was to give Jade a chance to spend some time thinking about whether she really wanted to go through with the marriage… To you.'

'Uh-huh. And whose idea was it for you to sleep with me?' he snarled, the fury starting to choke him again. How could he have been such a fool? To fall for their little scheme. Why hadn't he questioned much more vigorously all the things about the new Queen of Monrova that didn't fit?

Because you wanted her so damn much. That's why.

'No one's.' She gasped, looking genuinely shocked at the suggestion; why that should calm his racing heartbeat, he had no idea. He'd still been taken for a fool, by them both.

'I didn't… I didn't think we would hit it off the way we did.'

So that much at least had been real. His temper and outrage downgraded another notch. But her admission wasn't going to solve their main problem. He'd trusted her before he knew who she really was; he didn't trust her any more. And the only thing he cared about now— the only thing he could allow himself to care about—was preventing this mess from becoming a media scandal.

She sighed, drawing his attention to the soft swell of her cleavage over the towel.

The shaft of longing was echoed in the bright blush that seared her face.

He forced his gaze back to her eyes. He needed to figure out how best to handle this situation now. And he couldn't do that when the basic elemental need was still echoing in his groin.

'Does anyone but Jade know about this?' he said.

She shook her head.

'Are you sure? How the hell did you keep it a secret from Garland, and the rest of your staff?' he asked, astonished all over again at her recklessness.

'I suppose people only see what they want to see,' she said, the blush flaring over her cheeks.

Wasn't that the truth.

'You need to leave, so I can think,' he snarled.

She swallowed, her face a picture of embarrassment—which would have been oddly charming, given what they'd already done to each other, if the situation weren't so dire. 'Okay, would you mind staying here? So I can get dressed, and go back to my own rooms.'

He stepped back so she could pass him. 'I'll tell you how we're going to proceed tomorrow,' he said, just in case she had some idea he was going to let her run off without facing the consequences of her actions.

She nodded, but as she walked past him—her head lowered—he had to shove his hands back into his pockets, to resist the powerful urge to touch her.

But he couldn't resist the opportunity to admire the sweep of her spine and the soft swell of her backside, barely covered by the towel.

She opened the door, and glanced over her shoulder, catching him watching her.

Her blush ignited, while his own skin heated.

'I really am sorry,' she said. 'This wasn't ever supposed to get so complicated. I just wanted to give my sister a chance to live like a normal person, for a little while.'

It was a ludicrous thing to say. What did she even mean by live as a 'normal' person? How could Jade ever be normal, or Juno for that matter, when they were of royal blood?

But he stifled the urge to berate her further; there would be more than enough time to do that tomorrow. Right now his feelings were too damn volatile. He needed her gone.

'Get out,' he said.

He listened for a moment to her moving about in the adjoining bedroom.

Images of her dropping the towel tortured him and the heat in his pants became painful. He stripped off his clothing and stepped into the shower.

Taking himself in hand, he worked the strident erection in fast, efficient strokes under the punishing spray. After finding his release, he rested his forehead against the wet tiles.

When he turned the water off, the sound of her movements had gone. But as he began drying himself, while considering how best to deal with the fallout from tonight's events, he had the disturbing, but persistent thought that he was already anticipating seeing Juno Monroyale again in the morning.

CHAPTER NINE

'YOU'RE NOT SERIOUS?' Juno stared at Leo, her heart beating so fast it was threatening to leap right out of her chest.

'Do I look as if I'm joking?' Leo replied, the words bitten out in short staccato punches as if he were talking to a disobedient child who needed to be disciplined.

Nope, he definitely did not look any more amused than he had last night. If anything his uber frown had got a whole lot worse since she'd been summoned to his study this morning. She'd been up most of the night panicking about what he was going to do this morning, how he might choose to punish her... And Jade...

And on the rare occasions she had managed to fall asleep she'd woken again hot and sweaty, tortured by dreams in which Leo was the star player...

But of all the worst-case scenarios she'd envisioned during the night, what he'd just suggested hadn't even been in the top hundred.

'But... Why...?' she murmured. 'Why would you want to spend seven days alone in a secluded cabin with me? I thought you never wanted to see me again?'

'Because it's the only way to solve both our problems,' he said, not denying that he didn't want to see her again.

The foolish little bubble that had formed under her breastbone when he'd made the suggestion popped.

'I want you to stay out of the public eye until your sister returns, at which point you can swap back.'

Leo raked his fingers through his hair and she noticed the smudges under his eyes—and the shadow of stubble on his chin. So he'd had a sleepless night too.

Unfortunately, in a pair of dark jeans and a black sweater that clung to his impressive chest, he looked as hot as ever—which made the wave of sympathy tangle with the wave of sensation that had tormented her most of the night.

'I can hide in Monrova until Jade returns,' she offered. She couldn't spend seven nights

alone with him in a cabin—because the yearning, the need and, worse, the feeling of connection were all still there. 'Jade didn't have any
public engagements planned in Monrova over
Christmas—which was why it seemed like a
good time to do the swap.'

His eyes narrowed dangerously. 'If you're
trying to imply I put you at risk of discovery
because I persuaded you to come to Severene
for a state visit, you can think again.'

'Persuaded?' she said. 'You ganged up on
me with one of my father's advisors and prac-
tically kidnapped me.'

His brow lowered ominously. 'At the time
I thought I was kidnapping a queen. Not her
identical twin. If you had deigned to tell me the
truth, I would not have had the slightest inter-
est in kidnapping you in the first place.'

The cutting put-down sliced neatly through
her indignation.

'Well, anyway…' she said, scrambling to
shore up what was left of her self-esteem. 'The
point is if I return to Monrova now, I should
be able to keep well out of the public eye, until
Jade returns.'

Winning the blame game with Leo wasn't

going to happen, so it was probably better to stop playing it, because all it was doing was grinding what was left of her ego to dust.

'So you don't need to worry about my identity being discovered or causing a scandal.'

'Except that's not our only problem,' he said, the sarcasm in his tone as cutting as the earlier put-down. 'I didn't use a condom last night.'

His gaze skimmed down to her midriff, and the sensation that would not die chose that moment to swell between her thighs.

She wrapped her arms round her waist, assailed by the memory of his hard, heavy weight inside her.

Terrific. As if she needed any more reasons to feel lower than dirt.

'According to the internet research I did last night,' he continued, his hot gaze doing diabolical things to her already shaky equilibrium, 'we must wait seven days to take a pregnancy test to ensure we don't risk a false negative.'

'Okay,' she said. She wasn't going to be pregnant, she was sure of it. Even *she* couldn't be that unlucky. But even so… 'I could take a test in Monrova in a week's time and let you know the result.'

'That's not going to work for me,' he said, the flat tone tearing at what was left of her self-respect. 'Assuming you can even source a test there without the Queen's doctors finding out you're not the Queen, do you really expect me to trust you to get it done without screwing it up?'

'Yes?' she asked, hating the plea in her voice. And the slicing pain in her heart at his contempt.

Why had she let his approval mean so much to her, when it had always been conditional on her being the Queen?

'That wasn't a question, Princess.' The muscle in his jaw jumped, his lips pursing into a tight line of dissatisfaction. 'Just to be clear, I'm not letting you out of my sight until the test is done to my satisfaction.'

The rigid, uncompromising tone made her stomach hurt. The hollow ache was one she recognised.

'But what would we do? For seven days alone in a mountain cabin? When you can barely stand to talk to me?' she asked, her desperation getting the better of her.

She couldn't spend a week with him treating

her the way her father always had, like a reckless, unruly child who needed to be brought to heel. Not only would her ego never survive it, but she was very much afraid her heart wouldn't be able to survive it either.

He studied her, but then to her astonishment the tight line of his lips lifted into a sensual smile. And the disapproval in his gaze turned into something a great deal more disturbing.

'I can think of several ways to amuse ourselves that would not involve unnecessary conversation.'

'What?' Heat flooded up Juno's torso and hit her cheeks. 'You're not… You're not serious? You still want to sleep with me? Even though you detest me.'

And why was the hot spot between her thighs erupting like Vesuvius at the thought?

'I don't detest you. Unfortunately.'

'Gee, thanks,' she said, trying to channel her indignation and getting breathless instead.

Why was that foolish bubble of hope rising back up her torso? Because that was even more delusional than the volcano in her panties.

His gaze raked over her, the heat as caustic as the disdain. Then he shrugged. 'Obviously it would be your choice, but I see no reason not to explore the chemistry between us while we're there. There'll be little else to do, and that much at least was real.'

She stared back at him. She should tell him where he could stick his insulting offer. She should demand to know where he got off treating her like a disobedient child on the one hand, then suggesting a seven-day booty call on the other.

But the outrage and the anger got stuck in her throat, trapped behind that foolish bubble of hope. And something else entirely came out of her mouth. Something that had tormented her ever since last night.

'Why didn't you use a condom?'

The muscle in his jaw flexed, but his eyes widened.

'Was it deliberate?' she asked. 'Were you trying to get me pregnant so you could force me to marry you, when you thought I was Jade?' The accusation was so atrocious, she wasn't sure she even believed it herself, but something about his failure to use contraception didn't make any sense.

He was a cautious man. How could he have made that mistake?

Guilt flashed across his features, but it was accompanied by a wary tension that only confused her more.

'No,' he said. 'By the time I got my hands on you I wasn't thinking about anything at all. I would never do something so...' He stopped abruptly, his eyes narrowing. And then swore softly under his breath. 'Point taken,' he said.

'What point?' she asked. She hadn't intended to make a point.

'I guess you weren't the only one who got carried away last night,' he said grudgingly.

The bubble of hope under her breastbone pressed against her chest.

Perhaps he didn't totally hate her after all. Relief flooded through her. It felt like progress of a sort.

She tried to swallow down the bubble of hope but it wasn't going anywhere.

Hope was not her friend.

Things had got hot and heavy with Leo over the last week because he had believed she was a queen, and with majesty came great responsibility in Leo's world. But now he knew she wasn't, the pressure was off. Did that mean…?

'Okay, I'll go with you,' she said, the heat spreading into her cheeks as his intense gaze darkened.

'Excuse me?' he said, with the supreme arrogance that had always been a major turn-on.

'I can hack seven days alone in a cabin if you can.'

She could see she'd surprised him again when his brows launched up his forehead. But then he laughed. The sound husky enough to scrape over her nerve endings.

His lips twisted in a sensual smile that had the heat pulsating into her panties.

It was probably nuts to agree to go with him—she wasn't entirely convinced he didn't still detest her—but she didn't want things to end like this. She wanted a chance to show him the real her. And that the real her wasn't really that different from the fake her. That was all. Perhaps it was super self-serving, wanting to make up for the mistakes she'd made, wanting him to like her, at least a little, but so be it.

'You make it sound as if I was giving you a choice, Princess,' he said.

She'd begun to realise Leo always liked to have the last word.

He *had* given her a choice, though. The choice to jump him or not to jump him. And more importantly the choice to have this mean something, or not mean something.

This time she intended to make the right choice, on both counts, by sticking to one simple rule.

Hot was allowed, heavy never.

CHAPTER TEN

LEO CIRCLED THE Puma over the hunting lodge's heliport. The lights blazed from the luxury cabin's porch, illuminating the hot tub built on a platform under the trees, which had been fired up, as per his instructions.

Anticipation powered through his system as he brought the big bird down and switched off the ignition. Juno sat beside him. Her beautiful body, the one he'd had in his arms only last night, was cocooned in a ton of clothing topped by a heavy quilted jacket.

They hadn't spoken much since they had agreed to the trip this morning. But as he waited for the blades to power down, and his libido continued to rev up, he questioned his decision to bring her here, again.

All the arguments he'd given her this morning were real. Or real enough. But if this trip had really been about limiting the risk of scandal and making sure she took a pregnancy test, why the hell had he suggested they jump each other while they were here?

That hadn't been smart or sensible. It had been an impulse. And he was not an impulsive man. Well, not until he'd met Juno Monroyale.

Maintaining his anger with her would have been a whole lot safer... But as soon as he'd seen the dazed awareness in her eyes at his suggestion... The dangerous decision to indulge their baser instincts had come out of his mouth regardless.

The dusk lingered on the horizon, the stars already winking above the forest canopy. He should be exhausted, after all he'd had a virtually sleepless night, but even so, as she sat quietly beside him—for once silent—and he contemplated seven long days and nights alone with her, he'd never felt more alive, more alert.

She dragged off the headset.

'This place looks incredible.' The smile that tipped up her lips was both tentative and tantalising—a sign that she was as unsure about this as he was. But then one thing he had learned about Juno in the last seven days, she was a great deal more reckless than he was.

Which meant it was up to him to take charge.

'The landscape around here is so beautiful,' she murmured, the flushed pleasure on her face unguarded. 'I don't think I ever realised how much I missed my homeland until I came back.'

'How long ago is it since you were in Monrova?' he asked.

Her surprise at his question made him realise he'd never asked her anything about herself—even before discovering her true identity.

'Not since my father kicked me out of the palace at sixteen for molesting a king,' she said, the wry amusement in her tone sad somehow. So he'd been the cause, inadvertently.

'How did your father find out about that?' he asked.

'You didn't tell him?' she said.

'Absolutely not,' he said. 'Do I look like a tattletale?'

She sent him the quick grin. 'Actually, no, you don't, Your Majesty.'

He laughed, the chuckle strained as it rumbled up his chest. And it occurred to him he'd probably laughed more since he'd met her than he had in his whole life up to now.

Not helpful, Leo.

'We should get inside before we freeze,' he

said, pulling off his own headset, more keen than he should be to see her out of that shapeless clothing.

Climbing down from the cockpit, he grabbed their bags then helped her down.

He followed her along the path that had been cleared in the deep snow. With the helicopter blades finally silent, he could hear the crunch of their footsteps, and Juno's shallow breathing, the silence of the forest as night fell annoyingly romantic as the lights strung across the porch reflected in the fresh snowfall.

As they entered the lodge, he stopped on the threshold. His breath froze in his lungs as he took in the cabin's décor. It looked as if Santa had vomited over the luxurious furnishings.

Who had done this? He would have them fired.

'Oh, wow.' Juno's gasp of excitement broke through the chill seeping into his bones.

She spun round to take in the fire burning in the open hearth, the pine bows arranged on the mantel, and the six-foot tree in the corner festooned in fairy lights and red and gold ribbons and bows.

The musical lilt of her laughter echoed around the room, warming the chill in his chest.

'Leo, it's fabulous,' she said, before she spun to a stop. 'I didn't know you were a Christmas junkie.'

'I'm not,' he said, dumping the bags on the floor, the strange glow starting to disturb him. 'This wasn't my idea.'

'Oh,' she said, the smile dying—and he felt mean for ruining her moment of joy. Then annoyed with himself for caring.

'Are you hungry?' she asked, her eager expression only increasing the pressure in his chest. 'I could cook us some supper? I had a job as a short-order cook in a diner not so long ago. I'm pretty good.'

He frowned. Why would she have needed a job?

'You go ahead, the fridge should be fully stocked. I've already eaten,' he said, stifling his curiosity. He needed to get a handle on the feeling crushing his ribs.

'Is something wrong, Leo?' she asked.

'No,' he said, and watched the light in her eyes die. He refused to feel guilty about it. They were here to get through the next seven days, do the damn pregnancy test, hope to hell it was negative, then leave and never see each other again. Satisfying the chemistry between them was one thing, encouraging an emotional connection something else entirely.

Keeping things cool tonight made sense. They needed to establish firm boundaries before they enjoyed any fringe benefits. Juno Monroyale was a force of nature—wild and undisciplined. She'd captivated him without even trying when he'd thought she was a queen. He wasn't about to let her do the same now he knew she wasn't.

'I've got work to do,' he said, picking up his own bag. 'I'll take the bedroom at the back. You can have the master. Do you want me to take your luggage in there for you?'

'No, that's fine,' she said, extending the handle on her case.

He could see the confusion clouding her eyes.

'I'll see you tomorrow, then,' he said.

He was going to get through tonight without touching her, just to prove he could. Whatever happened in the next seven days, he was going to be calling the shots from now on. Not her.

But as he lay on his bed twenty minutes later,

staring at the wooden rafters on the lodge's ceiling, and heard her moving around in the cabin's state-of-the-art kitchen, the delicious scent of herbs and grilled lamb making his stomach growl, the memory of her bright smile and her little gasp of joy when she'd seen the Christmas decorations was still doing strange things to his chest.

Juno awoke the next morning to a white-out. The snow was falling outside the cabin in fat, fluffy chunks, covering the trees in a blanket of pristine white.

You never got pristine snow like this in Queens, and she'd missed it.

She showered and changed into her outdoor clothes and made herself some coffee, then headed out into the living room. She'd heard Leo the evening before in the kitchen making himself a midnight snack, had debated whether to surprise him. Then decided to let him sulk. Something had spooked him, something about the Christmas decorations. And it had made her sad to see it. Was it something to do with his mother's death?

She'd wanted to ask him more about it. But

ultimately she'd decided against it. She didn't want to break her 'no heavy emotions' rule on the very first night.

She switched on the Christmas tree lights—which she realised Leo must have switched off.

After rinsing out her coffee mug, she found a carrot in the fridge and headed outside.

Juno breathed in the clean, clear pine-scented air, the peaceful morning. The beauty of the snow-laden forest was a gift she wasn't sure she deserved but was determined to make the most of.

She formed a snowball, then began to roll it across the ground in front of the cabin. She hadn't made a snowman since she was eight years old, and she'd still lived in Monrova with her sister. They'd escaped from the palace every chance they got that Christmas, to escape from their overbearing governess and the sound of their parents arguing in the adjoining suite. They hadn't realised at the time it would be their last Christmas together. The snowman they'd made just before the thaw had been the last they would ever build. But Juno hadn't forgotten how.

'This one's for you, Jade,' she whispered as she set to work.

Thirty minutes later, she had lost the feeling in her fingers and toes, her jeans were soaked through at the knees, she'd discarded her hat and scarf and her anorak and was only wearing a thin camisole, because the sun was warm and building a snowman was a lot sweatier than she remembered it.

After perching another snowball on top of the larger, misshapen lump she'd made earlier, she retrieved the carrot and screwed it into the middle. She tilted her head to one side, to admire her handiwork, then grabbed her discarded scarf and wrapped it round where the head and torso joined together—calling it a neck would be a bit ambitious.

She stood back to check him over again.

He looks kind of grumpy.

'What is that?'

She swung round to see Leo standing on the porch, wearing nothing but a pair of sweat pants, some boots, a T-shirt, and a frown.

Heat infused her already sweaty body—and all the pheromones she'd put on hold the night before went into party mode.

How does he do that?

With his dark hair rumpled, the soft cotton outlining his impressive chest and his expression as sulky and imperious as it had been the night before, he looked good enough to eat. Or certainly nibble.

Relax, pheromones, and get a clue. He doesn't want you.

'Actually, I think it might be you,' she shouted back. 'He looks almost as sulky.'

'He?' came the distinctly unimpressed reply. 'That thing has a sex?'

'Yeah, I'm gonna call him King of the Grumps—sound familiar, Your Moan-esty?'

His brows rose, but then the frown was back. 'I'm hungry. How about you come in here and make me some breakfast?'

'Not until you ask me nicely.'

'Stop being contrary,' he demanded, as if she were one of his subjects. 'You must be hungry after all your...' he paused just long enough to be deliberately insulting '...hard work.'

How could he even sound suggestive when he was disparaging her perfectly good snowman? And why had her pheromones gone into party overdrive at the words 'hungry' and 'hard work'?

That was so wrong. On so many levels.

'Cook your own breakfast,' she said. She'd wanted to cook for him last night, but she was through sucking up to him. Sulking Leo might be sexy as all get out, but that didn't mean she was going to put up with his 'I'm the King of Everything' behaviour.

'Now who's sulking?' he said and turned to go back into the cabin.

Her temper spiked and, grabbing a fist full of snow, she flung it as hard as she could.

Much to her astonishment, because she'd always been a terrible pitcher in high school, the missile hit its mark, smacking into the back of his head and showering him in snow.

Oops.

He turned slowly, flicking the already melting snow off his damp T-shirt, the sulky frown now catastrophic. 'Are you mad?'

The giggle burst out of her mouth, part amusement, part shock, mostly hard-partying pheromones. 'You have a problem, King of the Grumps, come get me?' she said, then bent to grab some more ammunition.

Big mistake.

A freezing ball thudded into her chest, soaking the front of her camisole as soon as she straightened. And suddenly six feet four of enraged King was heading her way, stocking his own arsenal en route.

She shrieked and started pitching from behind the snowman.

It was a declaration of war.

Ten minutes of screaming, yelling, running, slipping, sliding, and some actual snowball-throwing later, and Leo scooped her up and threw her over his shoulder.

'That's it, I'm putting you out of action,' he declared as he headed back to the lodge, but she could hear the laughter in his voice.

She stuffed her last snowball down the back of his T-shirt.

'You little witch!' he roared, and shuddered violently, nearly shaking her off his shoulder.

She shrieked some more as he hefted her up the porch steps.

They were both breathless, laughing, covered in snow—well, she was covered, he was mostly dry, because her surprise pitching skills had totally deserted her as soon as war had been declared. He carried her into the lodge, scattering snow and ice onto the polished wooden floors. Then dumped her onto the large couch.

'It's payback time, Princess,' he growled. And the partying pheromones joined forces with the giddy beat of her heart as his gaze dropped lower.

Even wet and sweaty and flushed she is irresistible.

Leo's heart thundered as he took in the pebbled nipples under Juno's wet shirt. Was she braless? Heat shot into his groin.

Her riotous hair tumbled down around her shoulders. And her green gaze blazed with emerald fire.

He needed her naked, like yesterday. He'd woken up grumpy as hell, she wasn't wrong about that. After two nights of unfulfilled erotic dreams, was it any surprise? But he was through controlling his hunger—he'd established who was boss and that was enough.

He lifted her foot, tugged off one boot, and the other. Then kicked off his own boots as she watched him, the eager anticipation already firing through his system.

She hadn't objected to sleeping with him on this trip, so what was he waiting for?

The mood changed, from playful to intense. But it didn't matter. This was all about sex, always had been. Sex and chemistry and getting it out of their systems before they both went back to their real lives.

He lifted her and she wrapped her arms around his neck, hooked her legs around his waist and buried her face against his collarbone, her lips finding the pulse point beneath the stubble on his chin. Her scent—citrus and spice and warm, playful woman—surrounded him, her kisses so artless and enthusiastic his heart stumbled in his chest.

He staggered towards the lodge's master bedroom as he found her mouth. She shivered deliciously in his arms as they finally crashed into the bedroom together and he dropped her on the bed.

The frantic battle to divest themselves of their clothing took less than a minute but felt like an eternity as he watched her wrestling off her wet jeans, socks and panties and then tug the sleeveless T over her head. Her bare breasts bounced, the flushed nipples sending the heat pounding straight into his groin.

He stripped off his sweat pants and T-shirt and kicked off his boxers in seconds flat.

At last, they were naked, her eyes locked on his rampant erection as he grabbed the sweat pants and pulled out a condom with trembling fingers.

He ripped open the packet and rolled on the protection, aware of her eyes on him.

But as he climbed on the bed, and she scrambled back to give him room before lifting her arms to wrap them around his shoulders, he could feel his control slipping again. Grasping her hips, he pulled her under him, but as her hands fell to his shoulders, her eyes dark with a longing that matched his own, the shaft of longing—and desperation—was so intense, the squeeze in his chest so sharp, it began to scare him.

What was happening here? Because what should have been simple and straightforward sex, and nothing but sex, felt like more again.

He could see the glow of affection in her eyes, could feel their hearts beating in unison. She opened her mouth and the fear sharpened.

'Leo…'

He pressed a finger to her lips.

'Don't,' he said, his voice so thick with emotion it was starting to terrify him.

Her eyes became shuttered, and he had the strangest feeling he'd broken something that might never be repaired. But the hunger, the longing, the physical yearning leapt in to take its place.

He gripped her hips and flipped her over, then lifted her, until she was positioned on all fours, ready to be plundered. Need surged through him, the desire so strong he could hardly breathe. He didn't want to see her face, didn't want to see the emotion that he was terrified might match his own as he took her.

'Leo?' she whispered, her voice thick with arousal, but also trembling with need.

He nestled the rigid erection in the swollen lips of her sex, not penetrating, but stroking the slick seam, playing with her, to refocus her mind on what he could give her. Instead of what he could not.

She jerked, and he tightened his grip on her hips. He found the font of her pleasure and exploited it with the smooth strokes.

She sobbed, the guttural sound thickening his shaft even more.

At last, he could feel her shattering, bucking against his hold. He reared back, unable to wait a moment longer, and plunged to the hilt. The tight clasp of her sex milked him as she cried out. He moved, his thrusts deep, branding every last inch of her, revelling in her surrender. As her orgasm pulsed around him, his own climax built from the very reaches of his soul, shocking in its intensity.

The orgasm rushed towards him then slammed into him with the force and fury of a runaway train. He shouted out, the pleasure wrenched from him, and clung onto her slender frame as he let himself fall.

Juno lay like a limp noodle on the bed, Leo's big body covering hers, the scent of sweat and sex surrounding them, the imprint of him still humming in her tender sex. She closed her eyes tight, not wanting the blissful wave of afterglow to end. Not wanting to revisit the words she'd nearly blurted out.

Thank God he'd stopped her.

You can't go there. He doesn't want that.

She heard him shift, the words that had formed in her head, a declaration of need, longing, desire, replaying in her head despite her best efforts. But then a light kiss on her shoulder had her swinging round.

'Come on,' he said as he climbed off the bed. After discarding the condom, he reached down to lift her over his shoulder.

'Leo? What are you…?' She choked out a shocked laugh, pathetically grateful for his playful mood. 'Put me down! I'm exhausted.'

Not entirely true—getting a bird's-eye view of his naked butt from her position on his shoulder was having a restorative effect. And helping her forget about everything other than the sex.

'Tough,' he said. 'Now stop wiggling or I'm going to drop you.'

Pressing her hands against his back, she lifted up and twisted. 'Where are you taking me?'

'Outside.'

'You're… *What?*' She shrieked and began to wriggle in earnest as he pulled open the porch door and stepped out onto the snow-covered porch.

'Leo… Are you nuts? We're naked.' She carried on shrieking and wiggling, with him

laughing until she was dumped unceremoni-
ously into a pool of steaming bubbling water.
She slid under the delicious jets, letting the
water envelop her body, her senses as alert as
the rest of her. When she popped up, he was sitting beside her on the ledge of the wooden hot
tub, the steam bubbling up to guild his handsome features in a luminous film of moisture…
And smugness.

She slapped the water, covering him in the
steamy froth. 'You jerk,' she said, but couldn't
resist the smile at his outrageous behaviour.

'Hey,' he said as he caught her wrist and
tugged her towards him. 'It's Your Moan-esty
to you, Princess.'

She laughed as he dragged her up and over his
lap, until she was straddling him. Her shoulders
above the water felt the bristle of cold air, but it
only heightened the sensations rioting through
her body as his erection pressed against her
belly, and his heavily muscled thighs tensed
beneath her butt.

'I can hear you thinking,' he murmured as
he cradled her cheek with his palm, threaded
the wild spray of hair behind her ear. 'Stop it.'

She glided her thumb down the side of his

face, felt the delicious rub of stubble already beginning to darken his cheeks.

'Could I ask you a question?' she said as the curiosity overwhelmed her—she'd never seen him so relaxed or so open and it enchanted her.

He had forgiven her and there were so many things she wanted to know about him. Just small things, nothing major, maybe if—

'No questions, Juno,' he said, cutting off the eager thoughts. 'Unless they're about what I want for breakfast or how to construct a snow-man properly.' He captured her hand, bit into the swell of flesh beneath her thumb. 'Or when you want me to ravish you next.'

She could see the fierce determination in his gaze and hear what he wasn't saying.

They had six days together. Six days to ex-plore this intense physical connection. But deepening the emotional connection that had begun in the past week was out. Because all that would achieve was to hurt her more when they parted.

She swallowed past the lump of regret in her throat, forced herself to concentrate on the ex-hilaration of being in this beautiful place with this super-hot guy. And not the feelings threatening to hijack her breath and destroy her equilibrium.

It was Christmas, they had a week to enjoy this gift and she was not going to ruin it.

Or forget that by the time Christmas was over, what they had together would be over too.

CHAPTER ELEVEN

JUNO STUCK RELIGIOUSLY to the no questions rule as if her life depended on it in the days that followed, and developed a rhythm of sorts. She did all the cooking, because she loved to cook, especially for Leo, who it turned out had a voracious appetite, not just for her, but also for food.

The sex too was a revelation for her. She had never believed her body was even capable of this level of pleasure… And each day Leo ramped up the demands he made on her and she found herself meeting those demands with demands of her own.

For a woman who had always been outspoken, she'd never realised she'd had so little awareness of her physical needs, but with Leo there to tempt and tease and tantalise her, to wring every last drop of pleasure out of each encounter—whether it be fast and furious on the kitchen counter, or slow and languid in the shower—she began to realise what she'd been missing.

The more she fed the craving for him, though, the more she seemed to need—but what scared her the most was that the questions just kept multiplying.

And the more she contained them, the more desperate she became to know the answers.

To stop herself from breaking the rules, she badgered him into snowmobile rides into the forest, evenings in front of the fire, or card games to fill up the time when they weren't making love.

But even so, each night when he left her bed to return to his, after their last sex-capade of the day, it became harder and harder not to ask him to stay. And tougher still to wake up alone.

She knew why it had to be this way. Increasing the intimacy between them would be a lie, and she had to keep those questions at bay, to deal with the longing that clutched at her chest each morning when she woke to her empty bed.

Activity helped. So she established a routine for those empty mornings. Get up, get dressed, then head out to make another snowman.

Who knew she would discover she could be a morning person after all?

She loved the cold crisp mornings and building a snowman meant she didn't have to dwell on all the unproductive thoughts, all those questions she wasn't allowed to ask or all the emotions Leo stirred, which she couldn't acknowledge.

There were no more snowball fights. And she suspected she knew why, as each day the intensity of the sex, and the agonising tension of tiptoeing around all the things they weren't allowed to talk about, increased.

Leo didn't want to give her another opportunity to blurt out her feelings.

As those feelings had begun to terrify her, she was on board with that. Avoidance was definitely the answer.

Christmas morning arrived, and she built her last snowman—but there was no sign of Leo. She tried not to get upset or anxious that he was sleeping away this special day, when it was their last full day together.

Not a big deal, Ju. This is just an epic booty call. You've got no claim on him and the good news is he has no claim on you.

Luckily, she'd spotted a project that should keep her busy for most of the day.

Taking the turkey she had pulled out of the freezer the night before, she hefted it into the state-of-the-art kitchen. She was busy stuffing the bird an hour later when Leo's deep voice rumbled down her spine and his large hands settled on her stomach.

'What's that?' he murmured, as his face appeared over her right shoulder and he tugged her into his embrace.

'A snowman,' she said, aware of her pulse hammering too hard. 'What does it look like?'

He laughed. 'I thought as much.'

She twisted her head and smiled at him, her heart stuttering in her chest at the sight of his jaw darkened by beard scruff, his face so handsome her breath caught every time she looked at him.

Maybe they weren't a couple, but was it wrong to grab these moments of closeness so she could remember them when they parted?

Sympathy pulsed in her chest as she noticed the sadness in his eyes.

Christmas was hard for him; it was when his

mother had died. But she could fix that today. No questions asked.

She shifted out of his arms and reached into the fridge to snag the box of fresh eggs, the sliced ham and a quart of milk. 'Here, why don't you make us breakfast this morning while I concentrate on this?'

'Breakfast, huh?' he said, standing back and holding the produce as if he had his hands full of a couple of armed grenades.

'Yes, ham and eggs...' She frowned at his perplexed expression...as a strange thought occurred to her. 'Leo, you do know how to cook ham and eggs, don't you?'

'Why would I know how to cook ham and eggs?' he asked, as if she'd just asked him if he knew how to soufflé a pheasant or make sushi from scratch.

'Because everyone knows how to cook breakfast,' she replied. Unable to prevent the little jolt in her heart rate at what an endearing figure he made.

She'd never once seen Leo out of his depth. But that air of authority had slipped—as he stood barefoot in a kitchen, wearing boxers and nothing else, with his once perfectly styled hair sticking up on one side and his jaw darkened by a week's beard scruff, staring at the eggs and ham as if they might bite him.

'I've never cooked anything in my life,' he declared, as if that were perfectly normal.

'Not even an egg?' Juno asked, actually kind of shocked. She'd done all the cooking, but that was because she enjoyed it. She'd assumed he didn't—she hadn't realised he couldn't.

'Not even an egg,' he said without hesitation. He put the supplies on the kitchen counter. 'Why don't you cook as usual and I'll watch?' He gripped her wrist and pulled her into his arms, his hand landing on her butt under the silk robe she'd thrown on after her shower.

She snorted out a laugh, despite the leap of desire coursing through her sex-obsessed body. She'd become addicted to Leo, that much was obvious, but she knew a distraction technique when she saw one. 'Nice try, Your Majesty,' she said.

Drawing out of his embrace, she picked up the groceries. 'I've got a much better idea,' she added. 'Why don't *you* cook while I tell you how? It'll be my Christmas present to you, teaching you some basic cooking skills.'

She could see he wanted to object. And it occurred to her how tough it was for Leo to admit a weakness.

Up till now, Leo had been the expert. On everything. How to behave as a monarch, encouraging and supporting her while they were on her fake state visit. He'd even been the expert in bed, teasing out her pleasure and sending her senses soaring to heights she'd never believed possible. But now the tables were turned.

'You're not going to let this go, are you?' he said.

Juno's grin widened; this was one more precious memory she would be able to keep from their time out of time here. 'Nope.'

He swore softly under his breath. 'Fine, but don't blame me if you get food poisoning,' he added.

She laughed as she drew out a large metal mixing bowl from the impressive array of kitchen equipment. 'I won't.' She smiled at his frown and passed him an egg. 'Now let's break some eggs.'

'I think this has been my best Christmas ever,' Juno murmured, stifling a yawn, as she placed her bare feet in Leo's lap and relaxed into the sofa cushions, so tired and full of food she could barely keep her eyes open.

'It has been mine, too,' he said. The glow of firelight and the twinkle of lights from the tree in the corner of the room played over the planes and angles of his face.

Her heart expanded, the sincerity in his gaze making her chest ache with all the things she hadn't been allowed to say, but knew now to be true.

This was Leo with his guard down, the man without the crown who she'd only been allowed a few rare glimpses of before—while talking to a small child, at the height of passion, over a snowball war—and he was adorable.

Her heart pulsed painfully but she pushed the emotion to one side.

Sensation returned as he played with her toes and she thanked God for the timely distraction.

Don't ask for more, Juno. When this is all you can have, and all you're entitled to.

'Seriously, we cannot do it again. I'm exhausted,' she said as the familiar tug of desire centred in her sex.

His rough chuckle made her insides hurt.

'I never knew I had a foot fetish.' His smile warmed the ache in her heart. He dropped her foot back into his lap, caressed the instep. 'You have delicious feet, Princess.'

She grinned back at him, refusing to let the melancholy in.

The remnants of their Christmas feast—roast turkey, roast potatoes, a medley of vegetables and a red wine jus—lay on the coffee table where they'd devoured it after spending the afternoon and evening devouring each other in between bouts of industriousness in the kitchen.

Who knew Leo would look so cute learning how to make ham and eggs?

She resisted the tug of longing. They only had a few hours left—twelve at the most—before they would have to return to the palace. And Leo would be forced to don his crown again.

The unfairness of that pinched her heart, but she refused to let it in.

Not forced. Leo wore that responsibility willingly, because that was the kind of man Leo was. Overwhelming, tender, hot as hell, and loyal, but also damaged in ways she recognised, because she had been damaged in the same way. Never loved unconditionally, always knowing that, other than her sister, there was always a price to pay for affection. For approval.

Leo would never give up the throne—because his father had made him believe that was what gave his life value. And she knew that made a union between them impossible, because she knew she would always be second best. The way her mother had been, to her father.

She'd spent so much of her life resenting the monarchy. Resenting the choices her father had made, the decision to choose duty instead of family. In a strange way, being with Leo these past two weeks, discovering that she wasn't as rubbish at pomp and circumstance as she'd thought, had been a revelation, a confidence boost, a way of finally putting those demons to rest. That she could tame her recklessness, control her rebelliousness, if she was given the right support, the right help and guidance.

Look at me now, Father. I didn't disgrace you after all.

Jade had told her at the start of all this that she needed to come to terms with her past. Their past. All that she'd lost all those years ago. And she hadn't believed her. But her sister had been right.

She'd needed Leo, needed to prove she wasn't a nobody, that she was her father's daughter after all. And that should be enough.

Unfortunately, it wasn't, because she'd fallen hopelessly in love with Leo in the process.

A part of her wanted to blurt out the truth. But she couldn't, because however strong her feelings were, she knew he didn't return them.

She couldn't bear to expose herself again, to beg for someone's love and be rejected. To be told by another man she loved that she was not enough.

He stroked her feet with his thumbs, sending sensation shimmering into her sex, as he turned to her. 'Why did you get a job as a short-order cook?'

The pulse around her heart intensified at the off-hand question. She'd abided by his rules, and now... Did he know he was breaking them?

'Why do you ask?' she said.

'I just wondered if you did it because you enjoyed cooking so much.'

The question was loaded.

She could answer with the platitudes she had

always used before, when disguising the reality of her life in New York with her mother. And the financial fallout after her death. She shouldn't want Leo to know the truth, when no one else ever had. But the memory of what he'd called her on two different occasions came rushing back...

A spoilt brat.

And suddenly she wanted him to know that wasn't who she was. It was dangerous. Perhaps he wouldn't believe her, he might not even care, but he'd asked. And that was enough.

'I needed the money,' she said. 'By the time my mother died we were in a lot of debt. The penthouse had to be repossessed. I'd had a waitressing job at the diner since I was sixteen,' she added, seeing the stunned surprise in his gaze. 'But the cook's position paid more.'

'Why did you need money?' he said. 'Did Andreas not give your mother a fair divorce settlement?' He sounded outraged. Why should that mean so much?

'He did. In fact, he was more than generous. He wanted to be rid of her, and he was willing to pay,' Juno said, the familiar bitterness tightening her voice. 'But by the time we'd been in

New York for a few years, her drinking had become a problem. She couldn't hold onto any acting jobs, she'd lost her looks and the constant partying became an excuse to spend everything he sent her and borrow more. By the time I was sixteen we were in tons of debt.'

'Why didn't your father help you?' he said, straightening in his chair.

'Because she never acknowledged she had a problem and I'm not even sure he would have helped us if she had. He'd made it very clear that last summer in Monrova that I was a problem he didn't want to be bothered with either.'

She'd been too scared to ask, because she'd been sure the answer would be no.

Leo stroked her feet absently, his gaze locked on her face. 'Juno, that's appalling. I had no idea.'

Her throat thickened and she felt stupidly close to tears. To know that he believed her, that he cared, felt so huge. When it really shouldn't.

'Do you know what the toughest thing was though?' she said.

'What?' he asked.

'She still loved him. I always thought it was just drunken ramblings, when I'd be pouring her into bed, she'd say over and over again how much she missed him. How she wished she hadn't messed up. But I think now she really meant it. I guess it didn't matter to her that he had never loved her in the same way.' More than duty, more than scandal, more than his responsibility to the monarchy. 'Maybe if he had he wouldn't have discarded her so easily.' *Or me.*

'I am sorry I called you a spoilt brat,' he said, with a forcefulness that made her heart swell even as she acknowledged the dangerous parallels in her own life. She'd always known falling for Leo would be a mistake. Why hadn't she been able to stop herself? 'It seems that your childhood was a great deal harder than mine.'

'I doubt that,' she said. 'My father never hit me.'

'I should never have told you about that,' he said, his voice brittle with purpose. 'He wasn't a loving man, but I survived. And it taught me self-sufficiency.'

Did he really believe that?

She cradled his cheek, felt the muscle tighten in his jaw and her heart broke a little more.

They'd both said too much. But even if he regretted it, she never would.

'I wish I could have met that little boy,' she said, seeing his eyes becoming shuttered. 'I would have loved to give him a hug.'

'Don't...' He clasped her wrist and drew her hand down from his face. And she felt the deep sense of loss.

She shifted off the sofa, knowing she'd broken the rules, and paced over to the fireplace. She shouldn't have let that slip. Especially when she felt him step behind her, his voice husky.

'Don't be sad, Juno. That child is long gone.'

Is he...? Really? When you still tense at the sight of a few Christmas decorations?

She should leave it at that. She'd made a promise to herself she wouldn't beg. Wouldn't ask, so he could reject her. The way her father had.

But suddenly it all became too much. The need, the want, the heady emotion scraping against the raw spot he had revealed that still existed in her heart. And not telling him felt like the height of cowardice. What if all she had to do was ask? What if he didn't reject her, what if he loved her too?

She turned, to find him watching her. She gathered every last ounce of her courage and made herself tell him the truth.

'I've fallen in love with you, Leo.' The words released on a tortured huff of breath.

The flicker of shock in his eyes appeared before he could mask it and stabbed right into her heart.

CHAPTER TWELVE

'LOVE IS JUST a word. It doesn't mean anything.'

Leo hadn't wanted to say it, but what else could he do? The last few days—hell, the last entire week—had been torture. And the torture had only got worse. He'd known this might be coming, and he had dreaded it, ever since they had made love the first morning in the cabin and he'd seen the words she wanted to say in her eyes.

It had become so hard to stick to his own rules. But it was even harder to do so now he knew she was nothing like the woman he had assumed even a week ago.

She had continued to captivate and inspire him. But what the hell did he do with that, when he had nothing to offer her?

She blinked and swallowed. 'Is that all you have to say?' she whispered, the shock in her voice only making his desperation worse.

He cupped her cheek, drew his thumb across

the line of her lips, unable to stop himself from touching her, even though he knew now it wouldn't stop the yearning, it would only make it worse.

'We can't have any more than this week. I thought you understood.'

She pulled away from his touch. Her eyes darkening, the longing still there, but beneath it was the sadness.

'Why can't we?' she asked, so simply his insides turned over. 'I know you don't love me back, not yet,' she added, and the understanding in her voice pierced his heart. 'All I'm asking is that you let me in, Leo. Is that really so hard?'

She waited a beat, and the words were on the tip of his tongue. But the rush of emotion, of need, of yearning was so deep and visceral it terrified him.

He could not expose himself to that need, or it would leave him defenceless. The way he had been after his mother's death.

Something he had strived his whole life never to be again.

'Yes, I suppose it is,' he said, absorbing the desperate yearning he could not give in to.

'I see,' she said, a heartbreakingly poignant smile on her face. 'Thank you for being honest with me.'

She stepped back, the shutters coming down over her expression.

No. Damn it.

He grasped her arms, pulled her back into his embrace.

'Why do you need any of that, when all that matters is this?' he said. But he could hear the desperation in his own voice as he framed her face and pressed a kiss to her lips.

She opened for him instinctively. Their tongues tangled in a dance of desperation and desire. He felt her shudder of need. He tugged off her sweater and bra to reveal the full breasts, swollen with need. He'd devoured her body so many times already, why was it never enough?

He placed her on the sofa, stripped off the rest of her clothes and tore off his own, then knelt in front of her, to find the heart of her pleasure with his lips. She cried out, sobbed as he worked the slick, swollen nub, feeding on her pleasure, knowing exactly how to touch and tempt her to make her shatter.

This, he could give her this, why wasn't it enough? It had to be enough.

She rose up, bucking and shuddering beneath the sensual torment, her scent surrounding him, her surrender complete as the orgasm gripped her.

He rose over her, plunged the iron-hard erection deep into her welcoming heat, her sheath still pulsing with the brutal orgasm.

The firelight flickered over her body, the Christmas lights turning the chestnut curls to a mass of colours—her emerald eyes absorbing every ounce of his fear until all that was left was the need.

He plunged deep, took more.

He could not be the lover she wanted, could not let himself be that vulnerable ever again.

As her second orgasm gripped him, he felt his seed—hot, hard, unstoppable—gathering at the base of his spine. He pulled out just in time to spill it on her belly.

She lay exhausted on the sofa, her emerald eyes glossy with afterglow, but the sadness remained. He gathered his strength, to stand and lift her into his arms. She curled into his embrace, the shuddering sigh making his heart ache. He'd hurt her, and he wanted to make it right.

He carried her into the bathroom, switched on the power shower. And washed her with gentle, supplicant hands.

They stood together under the steamy water and he saw the water run down her cheeks, her expression so lost he couldn't tell if tears were mingled there.

She shivered with the emotional impact of their joining, and he felt like a bastard.

He placed her in the bed, and prepared to leave, but she reached out and caught his arm. 'Can you stay with me tonight? Just this once? I won't ask any more. I promise. But I don't think I can be alone.'

It was such a small thing, and so easy for him to acquiesce. So he broke his own rule and moved into the bed beside her, held her gently in his arms and felt her fall into a deep dreamless sleep.

But he stayed awake for hours, thinking of the young girl, left destitute by an alcoholic mother. And the boy, who might once have been able to open his heart to her—but had been lost long ago.

CHAPTER THIRTEEN

JUNO WOKE THE next morning, her body aching, but her heart hurting more. The bed was empty beside her.

She closed her eyes as the pulse of pain wrenched a hole in her chest.

She'd risked everything, and it hadn't been enough. When would she ever learn?

She was going to miss Leo. So much. And this beautiful Christmas. But it had always been a fantasy, a time out from reality, a moment she couldn't trust.

We can't have any more. I thought you understood.

Leo was a forceful man, and every inch a king, was it really any surprise it wasn't her he wanted?

He had so much love to give, she was sure of it, trapped inside him with that little boy, but she wasn't the one who could find it. And she had to accept that now, or she would end up like her mother, pining after a man who could never love her back.

She stretched, her body protesting slightly.

As if conjured by her thoughts, Leo appeared in the doorway carrying a tray laden with something that smelled delicious and her aching heart leapt painfully into her throat.

'Good morning, Princess,' he said.

Wearing nothing but boxer shorts, his hair ruffled, the scruff on his cheeks having turned into the beginnings of a very sexy beard, he looked like a man instead of a king.

She forced a bright smile to her lips. Maybe she couldn't have him always but now, today, this morning, he was hers and no one else's.

'Good morning, Your Majesty,' she said, dragging herself into a sitting position, and holding the sheet to her breasts, strangely shy as his gaze dipped to her cleavage.

He set the tray down on the bed beside her.

'Mmm…' She took a deep breath in of the aromas, trying not to let on that the last thing she wanted right now was food, her stomach too jumpy and unsettled. 'It smells really good. You're obviously a natural.'

But as she lifted the napkin he'd placed by the plate, she spotted the plastic stick in clear wrapping resting beside it.

Her jumpy stomach somersaulted up to her throat.

'I thought we could do the test after breakfast,' he said, matter-of-factly, as her stomach went into freefall.

How could she have forgotten this had always been the plan? And why did the thought of the pregnancy test feel fraught with so many more problems now than it had yesterday, before she'd blurted out how she felt?

'The instructions suggest it is best to do it first thing in the morning, when the hormone levels are strongest.'

She put the fork back down on the tray, her fingers trembling.

Maybe, if she were pregnant, he would want her? But as soon as the thought struck, she hated herself for it. A baby couldn't make him love her. And even thinking that would just make her more pathetic.

'If you don't wish to eat, I will understand,' he said with his typical pragmatism.

Why did the easiness with which he read her only make the yearning worse?

She nodded. He lifted the tray off and placed it on the side, then handed her a robe as she climbed off the bed.

She wrapped the robe around herself as he passed her the pregnancy test.

But as she reached for it, instead of releasing it, he pulled her close and cupped her cheek. His gaze roamed over her face, the affection, the desire, so bold and unabashed it only made her feel sadder and more inadequate.

'Whatever the result, we will deal with it together,' he said, his voice steady, his eyes kind. 'Okay?'

She nodded, and he placed a kiss on her forehead, then let her go.

It was the honourable thing to say. And she knew that he meant it, because he was an honourable man. But as she walked into the bathroom alone, the pregnancy test burning a hole in her palm, she knew that, whatever the result, it couldn't alter the fact he hadn't known who she was when they had made love without protection.

And he could never love her, even if he had.

* * *

Leo had never believed that one's heart could actually get lodged in one's throat, but something was definitely beating heavily there and threatening to strangle him as he waited for Juno to come back out of the bathroom.

He had tried not to think about the possibility of a pregnancy, had certainly not gone so far as to imagine himself and Juno parenting a baby. But as he showered in one of the lodge's other bathrooms and got dressed, he found himself imagining Juno's slender frame ripe with his child, and the tidal wave of possessiveness, protectiveness, was unmistakeable.

He tried to even his breathing as he waited on the bed they had shared twenty minutes later, the door to the bathroom still closed.

He heard the tap running, then cutting off. At last the door opened.

She stepped into the bedroom, still wearing the silk robe he had given her what felt like a lifetime ago, tightly knotted around her waist, the stick swaddled in toilet tissue in her hand.

Her head lifted and he could see the shattered shock in her eyes.

'It's positive?' he asked, but it wasn't really a question.

Her head bobbed. 'I… I think so. I reread the instructions several times.'

He strode across the room and lifted the stick from her trembling fingers. She looked so fragile, so he slung a steadying arm around her shoulder as he read the result for himself.

The wave of possessiveness peaked as he stared at the two clear blue lines.

'Yes,' he said. 'I read the instructions several times myself,' he admitted as he handed the stick back to her. 'Have you decided if you wish to have the child?' he asked.

Say yes.

He wanted to watch her grow heavy with his child, wanted to hold her and support her as she gave birth. But most of all, he wanted the chance to keep her by his side—warm, compassionate, honest, funny, forthright. Why had it never occurred to him that this could be a solution, not a problem?

He had wanted a queen. Why could that queen not be Juno?

She moved away from him and stood staring out into the snowy landscape beyond the bedroom. With her arms clasped tightly around her midriff, and her shoulders slightly hunched, he sensed her battle to hold in the swell of emotion too.

She seemed smaller somehow, and so young. This was a huge step for both of them, and something that had been forced on them by accident.

'You don't have to decide yet,' he murmured, his heart threatening to choke him as he waited for her answer.

She looked over her shoulder. 'I… I want to have it,' she said.

Even as relief washed through him, he could see the fear in her eyes.

He wrapped his arms around her waist and lifted her into his arms, ignoring it.

'Juno, I'm overjoyed,' he said.

Her eyes widened. The flush of stunned pleasure on her cheeks when he put her back on her feet made his heart stutter.

'Really, you're not angry?'

'Why would I be angry? We are to be parents. And Severene will have an heir. We must be married as soon as possible,' he said. He held her waist, the smile he knew was plastered all over his face echoing in his heart as her gaze met his, still uncertain, still wary. He touched her chin. 'Don't look so worried, this is excellent news,' he said, the possibilities suddenly endless.

He hadn't considered such an outcome, but now it all seemed so obvious.

'I will release a press statement first thing tomorrow. I expect there will be something of a diplomatic incident when we reveal the truth of your identity—and my chief of staff will have a cow when he realises he is going to have to arrange a state wedding in a matter of weeks instead of months. But when they hear about the child...' He pressed his palm to her flat stomach, marvelling at the thought of the child that already grew inside her. *His* child.

He wondered feverishly when she would start to show, when he would be able to feel his child kick.

'They will be overjoyed,' he said, stroking her stomach. 'There is no better press for the monarchy than a royal baby. Really, I could not have hoped for a better outcome. Once we have—'

'Stop, Leo.' Her hands covered his on her

stomach. And he was forced to raise his head. What he saw shocked him. The flush of pleasure was gone from her face to be replaced by sadness, and pain, the same grinding pain he had seen the previous evening—when he had been forced to tell her the truth, about what he could give her, and what he could not.

'We can't... We can't be married. You must understand that?'

'What?' The word came out on a broken huff of breath.

Surely he could not have heard that right? She was refusing him? Now? Why?

'Because nothing has changed,' she said.

'*Everything* has changed,' he said. 'You are having the royal heir, Juno. The future King or Queen of Severene. Surely you can see there is no other option now but for us to be married, so I can offer you and our child the full protection of the Crown.'

She stepped back, and his hand dropped from her stomach. 'It's not a king or a queen. Or an heir. It's just a baby. *Our* baby.'

'And as such it has a birthright,' he snapped, the anger surging to protect him from the pain. She didn't want him? When she had professed to love him? 'A birthright I will not allow you to deny.'

'What are you saying…?' She pressed a hand to her forehead, her distress so clear at the prospect it only hurt him more. 'That you'll take this baby away from me if I refuse to marry you?'

'Of course not,' he said. She was twisting his words, twisting everything around, making him into a villain, when he was simply trying to do what was right, for her and his child. 'But that doesn't alter the fact this child is the heir to the Severene throne. You might wish to shirk your duty and pretend you can be free from responsibility, but that isn't an option any more.' Frustration and fury rose up inside him, but beneath it lurked the empty space in his stomach, which told him without duty, he was nothing.

The pregnancy had forced his hand, and hers—and if she couldn't see that he would have to show her.

'Is that all this means to you? Duty? I don't want that for me or my child,' she said frantically. 'You told me yesterday you could never love me, can't you see that—'

'Stop it.' He gripped her arm, dragged her

back to him. 'Stop being so damn selfish,' he said, his fear now almost as huge as his fury. 'You're talking nonsense. Naïve romantic nonsense. This isn't about that any more.'

'Please, Leo, let me go,' she said, her voice breaking on the word.

He dropped her arm, the sheen of moisture in her eyes like a bolt to his heart. He thrust his fingers through his hair.

'Please, could you leave me alone, while I get dressed and pack?' she said, her voice so small and exhausted the bolt twisted.

He hesitated. He wanted to push the point, wanted more than anything to make her see how foolish she was being, but she still looked so fragile, so wary, he knew now was not the time. She was still in shock from the result of the pregnancy test. She needed time to come to terms with the reality of what this all meant. She was being rash and unpredictable and impulsive. Perhaps the pregnancy hormones were already affecting her reasoning? Who knew? This did not have to be decided right here and right now.

So he nodded. And tried to force himself to

relax. Now was not the time to demand and insist. He could do that later, if he had to.

What he wanted to do was pick her up and cradle her against his chest. Make love to her again the way he had last night. But that would have to wait too.

'Okay, Juno. Once you're ready we can head back to Severene. We can discuss things on the way,' he said, determined to make her see reason. 'There are many things about this situation I don't think you understand.' Things he would make her understand calmly and sensibly, once she'd digested the news.

She wrapped her arms around her midriff, as if she were shielding herself from him, and nodded. 'Thank you.'

It was hardly an agreement, but it would have to be enough, for now. Calling her names and losing his temper weren't going to make this situation any less volatile or easy to control.

Even though it was one of the hardest things he had ever had to do, he turned and left the room.

He headed straight to the lodge's study, to contact Severene's flight control centre so he could plot a flight path back to the palace. The sooner they got back, the sooner he could get Juno to accept—by whatever means necessary—that the only solution now was for her to become his Queen.

CHAPTER FOURTEEN

TEN MINUTES LATER, Juno crunched through the snow towards the back of the lodge. She shoved open the door to the garage. Her hands shook and her breath misted the air as she lifted the hood on the snowmobile Leo had used earlier in the week and ripped out the belt drive.

She pressed a hand to her abdomen, cocooned in the snowsuit.

A child grew inside her. A child who she could love. A child who would love her even if Leo could not.

What she had to do now was go home. Back to Monrova—which was less than fifteen miles across the border. And then back to New York. Back to her real life.

Her Cinderella story was over. He didn't love her, had told her he could never love her, and being pregnant with his child couldn't change that.

She hid the belt drive under a tarp at the back of the garage. Then she mounted the snowmobile parked nearer the entrance.

Frozen air filled her lungs as she drove the cumbersome machine out of the garage and hit the freshly fallen snow.

She headed past her family of snowmen and into the drifts that had fallen the day before—as she and Leo had made a Christmas feast together. And thought of that moment when she'd thought she could have it all, just by asking. What a fool she'd been.

She heard a shout from behind her. But refused to look back.

'Juno? Come back here. What the…?'

The curse words were muffled as the snowmobile headed into the trees and she revved the throttle to increase her speed.

What else could she do but run? She couldn't give him the power to destroy her. The way her father had destroyed her mother. Especially not when her child was at stake.

But as she sped into the forest, took the path towards the border, the tears fell freely down her face, chapping the exposed skin.

And she mourned, for a future that might have been real.

If only he'd been able to love her the way she loved him.

Leo swore loudly as he slammed down the snowmobile's hood. The words Juno had left for him on a notepad in the bedroom still echoing in his head.

Please don't follow me, Leo. I will be in touch. But I can't be your Queen. I'm so sorry.
J

'Damn it, Juno. What have you done?'

He ran into the house, the fury he had tried to keep at bay earlier, when they'd argued, starting to consume him. But beneath it was the black, agonising, all-consuming wave of fear.

How the hell was she going to navigate her way to Monrova, which was surely where she was headed? She didn't know the terrain, and she was pregnant, damn it.

Was the thought of being his Queen, of having his heir, really so terrible?

Grabbing the satellite phone kept in the

lodge's office in case of emergency, he stabbed in the number for his chief of staff at the palace.

'André, we need to send out search-and-rescue helicopters to the area on the Monrova-Severene border along the Aberglast pass. And deploy a ground team, too. Also, get in touch with the authorities in Monrova. We need to coordinate our efforts.'

'Your Majesty?' André sounded confused.

'You heard me. Princess Juno has run away and we need to find her.'

'Princess Juno, sire? Surely you mean Queen Jade?'

'No, I mean Princess Juno.'

'But, Your Majesty—'

'Juno has been posing as her twin sister for two weeks,' he interrupted the man's conversation. He didn't have time to explain this mess. None of that mattered now, if it ever had. 'Inform all the relevant parties of her true identity,' he said, his head starting to explode with the logistics of finding her.

'What about the media, Your Majesty?' the man said.

How ironic, Leo thought, that averting a scandal had once been his main concern. When it was the last damn thing he cared about now.

'I don't want them informed, yet,' he said. 'They'll only get in the way. The important thing right now is that we find her. She's pregnant with my child.'

But even as he said the words he knew the child was an abstract concept at this point. He had been overjoyed at the news of Juno's pregnancy less than an hour ago.

But suddenly, the child, its future, the monarchy's future didn't seem all that significant. None of that mattered any more. What mattered was Juno. And getting her back. Safe.

Didn't I pass this clearing an hour ago?

Juno brought the snowmobile to a juddering halt and assessed the terrain. The trees had all begun to look the same hours ago, but as she stared at the long shadows falling over the snow, she knew she'd been through this section of forest before.

Her hands ached and her arms were so heavy they felt like lead weights attached to her shoulders. She fisted her fingers, the cramps making the numbness painful. The cold had seeped into her bones hours ago.

The goggles began to mist from her body heat, so she thrust them up. The freezing air hit her chapped cheeks, increasing the pain.

She shouldn't have run. She should have stayed—Leo had been right to call her selfish.

Thoughts of Leo battered her tired brain—his face, so harsh, so handsome; his body, sculpted muscles, firm skin so beautiful she could feel its softness under her frozen fingertips; his scent, man and musk and sandalwood, invading her nostrils; his voice, low and husky and so confident about everything...

Why did I run? Why did I leave him?

He was safe, secure, strong. So much stronger than she had ever been. And warm; he could give her the warmth she yearned for. Except...

'We can't have any more than this week. I thought you understood.'

'If you can't behave yourself in a manner befitting your status, I will have you returned to your mother in New York immediately.'

The emotionless words—from so long ago, and only hours before—echoed in her head, becoming one voice, one man, one brutal reality that chilled her heart.

Leo didn't want her for herself. He wanted an heir, a queen.

Her father hadn't wanted her either. He'd wanted to protect the monarchy and to free himself of any scandal she might cause too.

The buzzing in her head became louder and she looked to the skies, to see a large black bird hovering overhead. She squinted into the setting sun, the frozen skin on her face prickling in the wind as the bird became wider, louder, its outline changing into something mechanical. Not a bird, a helicopter.

Snow flew up from the earth as she watched the mechanical beast set down at the far end of the clearing. The trees shuddered and shook, the bladed wings lifting the drift into a maelstrom.

Her mind blurred. Her heart pounded so hard the pain became one in her body, as the wings stopped spinning and a figure jumped out of the cockpit.

It ran towards her, a voice carrying across the frozen air. But the words made no sense, her mind too numb, too confused, too dazed to decipher what they meant.

'Juno, stay where you are. Don't move. I've come to take you home.'

Home?

But she had no home.

She watched, her body frozen in place, her mind spinning as the figure became a man running through the snow towards her.

His face became visible, blue eyes piercing, determined, full of accusation… Or was that fear?

Her heart slowed from a gallop to a crawl as he reached her. Flinging off his gloves, he cupped her cheeks; the warmth burned her skin and seared her soul.

'Juno, you little fool, you're freezing,' he said, the hot breath making her eyes water. 'Are you okay?'

But she couldn't make sense of the words, the pain so real and vivid now, the numbness starting to consume her.

Why had she never been enough? Why couldn't she be loved?

'Talk to me, tell me you're okay.' The voice begged, bullied, but it was so far away now she could hardly hear it.

She just wanted to sleep. To be warm again. To be safe. To be loved.

So she closed her eyes and let herself fall.

CHAPTER FIFTEEN

'IF THE PREGNANCY is weakening her, you must terminate it.' Leo grabbed the doctor's lapels, his fear starting to consume him. 'Do you understand me? I don't want you to take any risks with her life.'

'Yes, Your Majesty. I understand.' The doctor disengaged Leo's fingers, her eyes kind. 'But as I told you, the pregnancy is not an issue. Princess Juno had mild hypothermia. But we have warmed her body gradually, and are monitoring her vital signs and she should—'

'Why hasn't she woken up then? It's been nearly twelve hours since I brought her back to the palace.'

Twelve hours that had felt like twelve years as he'd sat by her bedside and willed her to open her eyes, to talk to him. To forgive him.

The fear had become so huge he hadn't been able to eat, or sleep. The truth was he was barely functioning.

He could still recall every minute detail, which had played over and over again in his mind since the moment he'd reached her in the clearing.

The way her eyes had lost focus, the chill on her cheeks, how she had gone limp and then collapsed into his arms. The flight home had been a blur as the terror that he might have lost her, that he had driven her to this, became too huge to control.

The hours that had followed had stretched into eternity as he'd struggled to keep the fear at bay, not leaving her side, as the doctors worked to keep her comfortable, to assess her condition. And she slept.

Why had he been too scared to tell her the truth?

'Your Majesty.'

He turned to see the nurse from Juno's bedside standing at the entrance to her room.

The terror engulfed him all over again.

'Is she dead?' he murmured, ploughing his fingers through his hair, the despair destroying him.

'No, Your Majesty, I believe she is waking up.'

* * *

'Juno, please wake up.'

Juno could hear a voice, a deep husky voice, beckoning her out of the darkness. Her eyelids felt so heavy, she didn't want to lift them yet, the lethargy that permeated her body so warm and comforting. But the voice was so insistent… And so familiar.

She forced her eyelids open, to see his face.

'Leo?' she whispered, her throat like sandpaper.

'Princess,' he murmured.

Where was she? And why did she feel so disconnected from reality? What had happened and how long had she been sleeping?

'You're going to be okay,' he said, his voice rough with purpose. 'And the baby too.'

The baby?

The only reason he wanted her.

The sharp blast of reality ripped through the fog and she blinked furiously, trying to stop the cruel memories flooding back, but it was already too late.

She looked away from him, the tears welling up now misting her view of the beautifully appointed bedroom.

She'd run, like the coward she'd always been. And he'd rescued her. She pressed her hand to her belly.

Her baby was safe. The baby she'd almost accidentally killed.

I can't marry you.

It was what she wanted to say. But the words refused to be released from her throat. The guilt and sadness were suddenly too much to bear. The tears flowed freely down her cheeks.

She had ruined everything. Perhaps this was a fitting punishment—that she would have to marry him now and live for the rest of her life loving him and knowing he could never love her in return.

Juno forced herself to look into his eyes, absorb his dishevelled appearance and the heavy beard.

She loved him, and she would marry him. And maybe one day he could learn to love her in return.

The silence seemed heavy as Leo took her hand and squeezed it in his.

'I'm so sorry,' she said.

At exactly the same time as Leo murmured, 'You must forgive me.'

He frowned then smiled, but it was a smile with no humour in it, only regret. The same regret that had wrapped around her heart.

'I can't imagine what you would have to be sorry for, Princess,' he said, the use of the endearment piercing her heart.

So many things.

'I'm sorry for swapping places with my sister,' she said, knowing the list was endless. 'I'm sorry for running. I'm sorry for putting our baby's life in danger,' she said, her heart so heavy it was hard to talk. 'I'm sorry for trapping you into a marriage you can't possibly want.'

The crease on his forehead deepened, the smile flatlining. 'Why would you think that?' he said, as if it weren't perfectly obvious.

'You don't love me, Leo. But you're being forced to marry me because of the baby and—'

'Don't.' He pressed a thumb to her lips to silence the rush of confession. 'Don't apologise for something that is lacking in me, not you.'

'I don't... I don't understand,' she said.

But instead of explaining, he lifted her hand, threaded his fingers through hers, and slowly brought her hand to his lips, pressing his mouth against the skin.

The prickle of sensation, the ripple of hope was almost more than she could bear. She could see the shadows under his eyes as he moved into the light. Why was it so much harder to face the truth of their situation knowing that he cared for her, just not enough? He stroked her knuckles with his thumb, finally lowering her hand and raising his gaze to meet hers.

What she saw there shocked her to her core.

This wasn't regret, or sadness, it was pain.

'Leo?' she whispered, her heart so full now she was scared it might burst.

What had she done to this strong, steady, beautiful man? What had they done to each other?

'It's not that I don't love you, Juno. It's that I was too terrified to admit it.'

The bubble of hope inflated against her breastbone, making the pain increase. 'But—'

'Please, let me finish,' he interrupted, but the roughness in his tone wasn't impatience, she realised, it was regret. 'I hadn't thought of a pregnancy, hadn't really considered how I would feel about it. What we would do. But when you came out of that bathroom with the positive result, everything inside me… It all felt so right. So wonderful.'

She nodded. 'I know, because you need an heir.'

He shook his head, the emotion in his eyes so real and vivid now the bubble of hope expanded even more. 'That is what I told myself. That is what I told you. And that is what I wanted to believe, but when you collapsed into my arms in the forest, I knew it was not the truth.'

'It wasn't?' she heard herself say.

'No.'

'What is the truth?' she asked, scared to hope now, but so much more scared not to know the answer.

'It's really very simple. I wanted to have a reason to demand you stay with me, that you marry me, without ever having to reveal my feelings for you. Feelings which I think began to develop the moment I first laid eyes on you at the Winter Ball.'

His head bowed, as if the weight of the world were on his shoulders. 'I told myself I didn't want you to love me, that I could never love you in return.' He traced his thumb over the back of her hand, then lifted it to his lips again in an act of supplication that stole her breath. And made her heart expand with the bubble of hope now bursting under her breastbone. 'The pregnancy was just another excuse. Not to confront those feelings.'

His gaze met hers, the shattered blue so full of longing her breath caught in her throat.

'And this is why you must forgive me, not the other way around. You told me you loved me, and I refused to say the same—refused to even admit it might be a possibility. Because I'm a coward. If you wish to have this child in New York, away from me, you can. I would never take the child away from you. Never force you to marry me for the sake of a duty you don't feel.'

'Oh, Leo!' She forced herself up on her elbows, to cup his cheek.

He was wrong. He wasn't a coward, he was just scared. She'd been a fool not to see that the love they shared—so rich, so sudden, so vibrant—had terrified him when it had scared her so much too.

They had both been terrified. And the only reason she'd told him first was because she'd never been able to guard her feelings. The way he had been forced to guard his.

'You idiot. Can't you see none of that matters now?' she whispered, her voice raw.

'It doesn't?'

'Of course not. Not if you love me too.'

He gripped her cheeks, pulled her towards him, until his lips hovered over hers. 'If being terrified of losing you is love? If wanting to listen to you breathe every day for the rest of my life is love? If wanting to go to sleep with you in my arms every night and wake up beside you each morning is love? If wanting to hear your voice, even when you are calling me an idiot, is love?' He placed his hand on her abdomen. 'If wanting to watch you grow round with our baby, and plant many more inside you, is love?'

She nodded, the tears cascading down her cheeks turning to happy tears at last.

'Then I guess I am in love too,' he said.

'Good,' she said. 'Now please shut up and kiss me, Your Majesty.'

EPILOGUE

Two days later

'*Your Majesty, is it true that the Queen is not the Queen?*'

'*Queen Jade, how are you in two places at once?*'

'*Which Queen is the imposter?*'

Juno blinked furiously, overwhelmed by the barrage of camera flashes and shouted questions that greeted her and Leo as they stepped onto the podium at the hastily arranged palace press conference. Her stomach jumped into her throat, the guilt threatening to make her vomit as she gazed out into the sea of faces—their expressions ranging from curious to astonished to stunned to excited.

She had caused this media storm. This was all her fault. She might even have destroyed the monarchy of the man she loved beyond reason, beyond…

But just as her panic threatened to outpace the breakfast she'd barely eaten an hour ago, as the advisors had briefed them on how to handle the news that Jade had appeared in Monrova that morning two days ahead of schedule, Leo's grip on her hand tightened and his arm wrapped around her shoulders.

Leaning close, he whispered in her ear, 'Breathe, Juno. It's okay.'

She glanced up at him and whispered back, 'Are you sure? Isn't this the disaster you wanted to avoid?'

But he didn't look angry or concerned, instead a grin split his features that made the warm glow in her heart intensify. 'Please don't remind me what a boring idiot I used to be.'

She smiled back at him.

While this love was still so new and scary, the thought of the baby growing inside her newer and scarier still, somehow she knew, with that look of bone-deep approval on his face, she could conquer anything. Not just her fears, but also her flaws.

They were all still there, of course, but somehow they'd lost their power to define her in the last two days. While she and Leo had talked and laughed, and made love, and he had reassured her constantly that, whatever happened next, he had her back.

She'd been alone for so long, it felt strange knowing that she wasn't any more. She knew it would take her a while to fully accept it. But all he demanded of her, because he was as astute as he was wonderful, was that she concentrate on believing him.

'Are you sure you don't want me to handle this alone?' he murmured as the palace press officer announced them and attempted to silence the crowd of over-eager journalists. 'I don't want you overtaxed,' he added.

She shook her head. 'I got us into this fix, I think it's up to me to help get us out of it, don't you?'

He pressed his forehead to hers, in a gesture so full of love and affection her heart expanded in her chest. The room went quiet, the world's press holding their breath. 'We got into this fix together, Juno. Don't ever forget that. And it's a fix I will be grateful for, for the rest of my life.'

He kissed her softly, and she kissed him back, not caring as the barrage of camera flashes and shouted questions went off again.

Her skin had heated to what she thought was probably an impressive shade of scarlet as Leo turned to the assembled crowd and—having waited for everyone to finally quieten down again—addressed them.

'I have a statement to make on behalf of myself...' he sent Juno a smile so full of love she was surprised she didn't start floating '...and the woman I very much hope will become my Queen. Eventually. But first of all I should introduce her to you properly. Her name is Princess Juno Alice Monroyale, and I love her unconditionally.'

The room erupted again, the inevitable questions being fired at them both. Juno felt her heart swell to impossible proportions as the press officer attempted to outline the arranged explanation that had been agreed with Jade and her advisors that morning—that Juno and her sister had swapped before the Winter Ball to give Jade a break from her royal duties, Leo had been in on the ruse, but then he and Juno had fallen hopelessly in love.

As the questions followed, Leo answered most of them, but when he deferred to her, his hand in hers and his presence beside her made her aware that, no matter what she said, or how she said it, he wouldn't stop loving her, or supporting her.

It was a heady feeling. And one she intended to spend the rest of her life getting used to.

After ten minutes, the time limit Leo had insisted on, the press officer brought the conference to a close. And then a screen behind the stage lit up with Jade's press conference in Monrova, which had been timed to coincide with theirs.

That was their cue to leave.

Leo ushered her backstage, then led her through the crowd of advisors—ignoring every one of their attempts to waylay them—and into his private study.

He slammed the door, leaving them alone together, then gathered her into his arms.

'Thank God that's over with,' he said, his mouth lowering to hers. 'Now I plan to spend the rest of the day ravishing you.'

A delighted giggle escaped before she could stop it, but as his mouth lowered to hers she stifled the yearning and pressed her palms to his chest. Something that had been bugging her since her phone call with Jade that morning niggled at her again.

'Leo, wait. I'm worried. I think something's going on with Jade.'

He lifted his head, his lips twisting into the tantalising grin she had become totally addicted to.

'Uh-huh.' He nuzzled the spot under her ear that he knew would drive her wild. 'You mean apart from the fact...' his lips travelled down, trailing fire in their wake to land on her collarbone '...that she's been playing hooky for three weeks in New York...' Juno gasped as his hand drifted under her blouse to tantalise the place on her back he now owned unconditionally while his lips kept wreaking havoc on her pulse point '...while the man she was supposed to be marrying has fallen in love with her incorrigible twin.' His roving hand slid down the back of her jeans.

The laugh at his behaviour choked off in her throat, but the niggling guilt refused to go away.

'No... There's something else...' Juno's breathing became staggered as she tried to keep her mind and her hormones on track under Leo's relentless onslaught. 'When we talked this morning, she seemed…sad. And she didn't tell me why she came back from New York two days early.' It was the reason why they had been forced to arrange a press conference so suddenly. The cat—or rather the Queen— had suddenly been out of the bag. 'I'm worried about her,' Juno admitted. 'I hope I didn't screw things up for her with this swap—when every- thing turned out so brilliantly for us.'

Leo leaned back and sighed. He dropped his forehead to hers. His hands stilled. 'You know what I think, Juno?'

'No, what?' she said.

'Your sister is a grown woman and an ex- tremely competent queen. *If* there's anything she needs to tell you, she will, because she loves you and she knows you love her. I adore your compassion but sometimes you just have to give people space.'

'Are you telling me to back off and stop being so nosey?' she asked, the guilt releasing its grip on her throat. Leo was right. Jade was smart and sensible and she knew Juno had her back. If Jade needed her, she'd let her know.

He smiled. 'That too.' He lifted her into his

arms as the giddy laugh popped out after all. 'Now let's start celebrating the new year early.'

She held on to his shoulders and found his lips with hers.

Ready to celebrate this new year, and the next, and all the years to come as soon as humanly possible.

* * * * *

LET'S TALK
Romance

For exclusive extracts, competitions
and special offers, find us online:

📘 facebook.com/millsandboon

📷 @millsandboonuk

🐦 @millsandboon

Or get in touch on 0844 844 1351*

For all the latest titles coming soon,
visit millsandboon.co.uk/nextmonth

Want even more
ROMANCE?

Join our bookclub today!

'Mills & Boon books, the perfect way to escape for an hour or so.'

Miss W. Dyer

'Excellent service, promptly delivered and very good subscription choices.'

Miss A. Pearson

'You get fantastic special offers and the chance to get books before they hit the shops'

Mrs V. Hall

Visit millsandbook.co.uk/Bookclub and save on brand new books.

MILLS & BOON